C000253748

THE THIEF

JAN NEEDLE

Resource Material
Vivien Gardner
and Stephen Cockett

Series Consultant
Cecily O'Neill

CollinsEducational

An imprint of HarperCollins*Publishers*

Copyright © 1990 Jan Needle, Viv Gardner and Stephen Cockett

First published 1990 by CollinsEducational
An imprint of HarperCollins*Publishers*
77–85 Fulham Palace Road
Hammersmith
London W6 8JB

Reprinted 1991, 1992

ISBN 0 00 330237 7

Acknowledgements

Illustrations: Garry Fry/Kidbrooke School, London, cover photograph; Hemesh Alles, pp 40–41, 46–47, 60, 63, 64, 73, 86, 91; Metropolitian Borough of Stockport Reference Library, p 52; Chislehurst Caves, p 53; Nottingham County Library Service, p 54; Stockport Express Advertiser, p 58; Stockport Messenger, p 59; The J. Allan Cash Photolibrary, pp 65, 72; Camera Press London, pp 70, 88 (photographer Lionel Cherrault); Fleetway Publications, pp 77 and 78 (top); D.C. Thomson & Co Ltd p 78 (btm); Cathy Dineen, pp 81, 83; Brian Merrick pp 83, 90; Rada Robinson p 83.

Text extracts:
Stockport Express Advertiser, pp 58, 59 (btm); Stockport Messenger, p 58 (top); Exeter Weekly News, pp 61, 88; *The Experience of Prison*, ed. David Bell, Longman, 1977, p 63 ('A Prisoner's Wife'); *The Frying Pan*, Tony Parker, Hutchinson, 1970, c/o Rogers, Coleridge & White Ltd, pp 65, 69, 70; The Daily Mail, p 68; The Home Office, p 71 (graph); *The Human Zoo*, Desmond Morris, Jonathan Cape, 1969, p 84 (a–g), The Daily Star, p 85; *Recording Children's Progress*, Joan Dean, 1972 (school report) p 87.

Typeset by Northern Phototypesetting Co Ltd, Bolton
Printed and bound in Great Britain
by Bell & Bain, Glasgow

CONTENTS

THE CHARACTERS

KEVIN PELHAM — A schoolboy. His family are skint, and it shows.

TRACEY — His sister. About sixteen. Shop assistant.

MUM — Careworn, prone to depression, takes Valium.

JENNY — Kevin's friend.

BUZZ — Ditto.

TIM ATKINSON — A youngish teacher, pleasant and concerned.

JUDY SMITH — Ditto.

MISS WARING — School librarian. Likes Kevin.

MR BUTLER — A fat and pompous teacher. Dislikes Kevin.

PADDY — Junk shop owner. Middle aged and kind.

BOB — A thief.

ALAN — Ditto.

JACK — A thief, but more violent and dangerous than other two.

KIDS AT KEVIN'S SCHOOL, including:

Pupil

Girl One

Girl Two

Girl Three

The Thief

TEACHERS AT KEVIN'S SCHOOL

POLICE

N.B. On TV, Paddy was black. In a school production, all the characters can be any colour, naturally.

THE THIEF

SCENE ONE

*A school corridor between lessons. There is an enormous babble of voices, and a buzzer sounding loudly and insistently. The kids push, shove and shout until **Jenny** emerges into view. She is looking for someone.*

JENNY *waving* Buzz! Hey, Buzz! Over here!

A pupil pushes past her.

PUPIL Get out of it.

JENNY *automatically* Get knotted. *Calls* Buzz!

***Buzz** emerges from the crush and sees her.*

BUZZ Jen!

As he pushes forward, he bangs into a couple of girls.

GIRL ONE Do you mind?

GIRL TWO Rude pig.

BUZZ *grinning* Sorry.

*As he extricates himself, **Jenny** moves towards him. The babble is gradually diminishing.*

JENNY Come on. We'll miss it.

He reaches her.

BUZZ It gets worse, doesn't it? It's like a madhouse.

GIRL THREE *passing* Speak for yourself!

***Jenny** sticks her tongue out at the retreating back. The crowd is thinning out.*

BUZZ *to **Jenny**, not meaning it* She fancies me.

JENNY Where's Kevin? I thought he was with you.

BUZZ Me? No, haven't seen him. He doesn't do French. He can't speak English yet!

There are only a couple of stragglers now. The babble is almost gone. Only the buzzer remains loud.

1

JENNY   I said to meet us here. I saw him before break. He can't be knocking off again.

The buzzer gives a final blip, then stops. They are alone.

Buzz   He courts trouble, my Mum says. He goes looking for it. Come on, Jenny, we'll be late.

*He begins to leave. **Jenny** hangs back.*

JENNY   *unsure*   Yeah. No need to drop ourselves in it too, is there?

BUZZ   Come on, then. Jenny!   *Brief pause*   Look, if he comes he comes. We can't hang on any longer.

JENNY   But you know old Butler. If Kevin skips his history he'll murder him. Why does he *do* it?

***Buzz** is almost gone.*

BUZZ   Jenny. There's just no point.

She shrugs, and follows him.

JENNY   No. He's crazy, honestly. Nuts.

*When they have gone, we become aware of **Kevin,** who has been standing alone and unseen, well away from them. He does not move, just stands. Then he turns and leaves. Blackout.*

SCENE TWO

The staff cloakroom. There is a line of coats on a horizontal rail, with someone rooting among them. From behind, it could be Kevin — the same minimal school uniform of grey trousers and shirt, and blue jumper. The face is hidden in the coats.

*Then a lavatory flushes, and the figure freezes. It scrabbles with something in its hands, and a wallet is dropped to the floor. The figure stoops to retrieve it, thinks again, and turns to run. In one hand is a banknote. Full face, we see that it is not Kevin. **The thief** runs out.*

*From behind, a teacher — **Tim Atkinson** — emerges, looking puzzled.*

MR ATKINSON   *calls*   Hallo?

He comes to the front of the coatrack and sees the wallet on the floor. He picks it up.

MR ATKINSON   What's going on?

He moves rapidly to the door and looks up and down the corridor. Nothing. He flips open the wallet and looks at the name and address in the clear window.

MR ATKINSON   Judy Smith's. I wonder if anything's gone . . .

SCENE THREE

The School Library. **Kevin** *is sitting at a table, looking at a large old book, and copying parts of a map on to paper beside it. Behind him, with a pile of books in her hands, is the Librarian,* **Miss Waring.**

MISS WARING   It's a good one, isn't it, Kevin? It's the clearest map of the caves I've ever seen. I thought you'd like it.

KEVIN   Yeah. Thanks, Miss. It's brilliant.

MISS WARING   You shouldn't be looking at it now though, should you? You could get into trouble.   *Brief pause   I* could get into trouble!

KEVIN   *quickly*   No, Miss. I'm meant to be here. I'm on library.

MISS WARING   *not upset*   You're telling lies again, as well. You can't be due here now, because it's my free period. What lesson are you meant to be in really?

Kevin *looks down.*

KEVIN   History. Miss, you won't tell Butler will you? I hate him.

Miss Waring *turns away to hide a smile. She puts on a sonorous, Butler-like voice.*

MISS WARING   "This boy has hissed all his mystery lessons and tasted three worms." Do you know who said that?

KEVIN   *not caring, either — it's not a very funny joke, he thinks*   Miss?

3

MISS WARING   It was Doctor Spooner. It's a Spoonerism. He wrote it as a school report, last century, but got it wrong. This boy has missed all his history lessons and wasted three terms.   *Brief pause*   Some people think it's funny.

KEVIN   You won't tell him though, will you, Miss? Mr Butler? He thinks I'm thick. He thinks history's war and stuff. He doesn't even know about the caves. I hate him.

Pause

MISS WARING   Kevin, you've got twenty minutes left, all right? You can copy your maps and you can keep your mouth shut. But if you expect me to lie to teachers for you, you're . . . well.

KEVIN   He won't care. He won't miss me. He'll be glad.

Miss Waring has turned away.

MISS WARING   As far as I'm concerned, you're invisible. Just shut up and leave me alone. But if I'm asked, Kevin — I tell the truth. OK?

Pause

KEVIN   Yeah.

SCENE FOUR

A street corner. **Buzz, Jenny** *and* **Kevin** *are having a discussion, huddled up against the cold. All in anoraks,* **Buzz** *with his small rucksack over his shoulder. Other kids might be mooching past. It's the end of afternoon school.*

JENNY   But where did you get to, Kev? We waited ages.

KEVIN   I had the gut-rot, didn't I? We had a takeaway last night. It gave me the runs.

JENNY   They must've been the marathons. You were away for Butler's whole lesson.

KEVIN   Yeah. I bet I didn't miss much, though. What a berk.

BUZZ   He missed *you*.   *In Butler's voice*   "Mr Pelham has not deigned to be with us again, I see. What that boy knows about history would fill a very small book indeed."

KEVIN I bet I know more than him about some history. *Real* history. I went to the library and read up on the caverns.

Jenny and Buzz don't like the subject of the caverns much. Jenny tries to slide over it with a joke.

JENNY Pull the other one! You don't even know where the library is!

BUZZ Anyway, mate, Butler thinks you were skiving off, whatever your story is. You'll end up in detention, probably.

KEVIN I've got an alibi! I was in the library twenty-five minutes! She'll say!

BUZZ Brilliant. And Butler's lesson was thirty-five, divvy. Some alibi.

JENNY Anyway, knock it off about the caverns, right? They're private, and they're dangerous, and you've been warned. We all have.

BUZZ Dead right. One more time, and *finish*. My Mum says that if——

KEVIN *interrupts* Never mind your Mum, OK? Because we're going down again. We're going down today. And this time — we're going to find some stuff. Treasure.

Jenny and Buzz make exaggerated gestures of despair/ amazement. They've heard all this before, with knobs on.

JENNY Oh my God. Here we go again.

BUZZ Kevin, for crying out loud! Play another record, mate.

KEVIN *eagerly* Look, I'm telling you! I found a new map in the book Miss Waring gave me. There's new bits. Bits that even *I* don't know about. There's a bomb store that's completely cut off from the rest. It's completely secret.

JENNY So why should it have treasure if it's a bomb store? Bombs aren't treasure. That's ridiculous.

KEVIN But there'll have been people working down there. In the war. Hundreds of them. There's only one way in and no way out. They're bound to have left something. Lost things.

Pause. He is heated, they are fed up with him. **Buzz** *settles his rucksack on his shoulder to leave.*

BUZZ You've lost something, mate. You've lost your marbles. If it was a bomb store, they'll have cleaned it out, won't they? They're not bananas. Bombs are *bombs*.

KEVIN But it's worth a try! No one's looked at it for years! We've got to go and have a look, we've got to! Jenny!

She looks at her watch and shivers.

JENNY Look, I've got homework, and it's nearly time for tea. I'm freezing.

KEVIN But it's warm down there. A constant fifty-five. Come on.

BUZZ *mocking* What's fifty-five when it's out? In Celsius?

KEVIN *sulkily* This book said fifty-five, it's old. How should I know? Anyway, it's warm. You know it's warm.

BUZZ Not as warm as home, though. Coming, Jen?

KEVIN Look, Jenny. Give it one more go, eh? We'll find the new bits. And if there's nothing, we'll . . . well, that'll be it, won't it?

JENNY Not tonight, Kev. I'm cold. It's going to be dark soon.

KEVIN Just half an hour. Look — tomorrow, then? The weekend. *They won't look at him* Oh, what the hell! You're yellow, both of you! Chicken!

He suddenly runs off.

JENNY Kev! Kevin! *To* **Buzz** Oh well. At least he's not gone to the caverns. I bet he'll go home and do his maps. Oh well.

They stand for a moment, wondering what to do.

BUZZ D'you think he really believes it, though? All that treasure rubbish? It's so *babyish*.

JENNY He lives in Cuckoo-land. It's the same about his Dad.

BUZZ *half laughs* Yeah. What's he meant to be this time? A deep-sea diver in the Middle East? A ruddy jailbird.

6

They begin to walk. **Jenny** *ponders.*

JENNY   Maybe he needs to make things up. Maybe it makes him feel better. And a bit of spare loot would certainly come in handy for them, wouldn't it?

BUZZ   He's not a baby, though, is he? Making all that stuff up. I mean, for crying out loud. A ruddy *jail*bird.

They have gone.

SCENE FIVE

The Staff Room.   **Tim Atkinson** *and* **Judy Smith** *are on their own at one side. Two or three other teachers in chairs, marking, or preparing to go home.*

MISS SMITH   *with wallet in hand*   I'm not absolutely certain, Tim, but I think it's a fiver. I'm pretty sure I had four. And you actually saw someone?

MR ATKINSON   Heard. Sorry. But I must have disturbed them if they didn't take the lot.

MISS SMITH   It must've been a kid, too. The credit cards are all there. Aren't they little swine?

MR ATKINSON   *joking*   Some would say it served you right for leaving your wallet in your coat pocket.

MISS SMITH   Some would get a smack in the mouth.   *Brief pause*   I shouldn't have, though, you're right. I didn't mean to.

MR ATKINSON   Ah well. If it's only a fiver.

A fat and pompous teacher has entered.   **Mr Butler.**   *He passes close by them.*

MISS SMITH   It's the principle though, isn't it? I mean — they ought to be caught or they'll do it again. I suppose we could ask around. Someone might have been on the loose from their class.

MR BUTLER   What was that, my dear? Looking for a runner, are we? An abscondee?

Judy Smith *and* **Tim Atkinson** *exchange glances. They do not like* **Butler.** **Judy Smith** *puts her wallet into her bag, but he has noticed it.*

MISS SMITH   It's nothing, thank you, Mr Butler. Just a thought.

MR BUTLER   Do what again, exactly? Did I hear you say that someone should be caught?

MR ATKINSON   No, sorry. Come on, Judy.

MR BUTLER   Well if I am correct in linking the wallet with the missing person, my dear, look no further. Kevin Pelham. Ask him for whom the history bell tolled this afternoon — it was not for he. He was notable only for his absence, which at least made a pleasant change. Filching from wallets, was he? That's about his mark.

Judy Smith and Tim Atkinson edge for the door, embarrassed.

MISS SMITH   Look, honestly, Mr Butler.

MR BUTLER   He's a terrible little thief, you know. Just like his father. Check his pockets. That's what I'd do.

As they leave, Miss Waring comes in, carrying books. Tim Atkinson knocks one out of her hands.

MR ATKINSON   Sorry. Bit of a rush. You know.

He makes a face to indicate he's having trouble with Butler, and leaves with Judy Smith. The Librarian kneels to recover the book.

MR BUTLER   Unmannerly swine, aren't they? Typical of the new breed of teacher. No wonder the children are such louts.

Miss Waring deliberately does not reply.

MR BUTLER   Talking of louts. Have *you* seen Kevin Pelham this afternoon?

She stands up and faces him, coolly. She makes her decision.

MISS WARING   No, Mr Butler. I have not.

MR BUTLER   It was just a thought. He'd rather do anything than work, of course — even read a book! I suppose you keep the *Beano* in the library in this democratic age?

She faces him, with dislike.

8

MISS WARING   Kevin Pelham, as it happens, is quite a keen reader. Of history books. And I don't think he's a lout, either.

Although a bully, **Butler** *is no coward.*

MR BUTLER   *sarcastically*   Oh, do you not? Well well, how interesting. But then you, Miss Waring, are like that other pair, are you not? You have rather a lot to learn.

Miss Waring, books in hand, walks away from him. She turns her head, with contempt.

MISS WARING   If I have, Mr Butler, I don't think you're the one to teach me. Anything.

SCENE SIX

Kevin's bedroom. **Kevin** *is sitting on his bed working at a large map of the caverns, with felt-tip pens. His* **Mother,** *a tired-looking woman in her late thirties, is in the doorway. A small transistor is playing loudly.*

MUM   Kevin, turn it off and do your homework.

Kevin gestures at the map with a pen.

KEVIN   I am. This is my homework.

MUM   What? I can't hear myself think.

She comes into the room and switches off the radio. From outside we hear the TV, loud.

KEVIN   Aw, Mum. Leave it on. I can't concentrate. Anyway, you watch telly all the time.

MUM   Don't you be so cheeky. You've got to do your work. Put that map away and get on with your homework.

KEVIN   I told you. This is my homework.

MUM   You're lying, Kevin. Stop *lying*. It's that game. That dungeon game. You're always playing it.

KEVIN   It's geography. It's a special map I've got to do. For a project. I could win a prize!

Pause. **Mum,** *exhausted, sighs. She's heard all this before.*

MUM *sadly and quietly* You're so much like your father, Kevin. Stop *lying*. You're so much like your Dad . . .

SCENE SEVEN

A cafe table. **Miss Smith** *is sitting with* **Tracey**, *Kevin's seventeen-year-old sister, who is wearing a white shop assistant's coat.*

TRACEY I nearly had a heart attack, that's all. It's a good job I wasn't up the ladder when you came in.

MISS SMITH Yes, I'm sorry. I wouldn't have troubled you at work at all, but I couldn't think of any other way. I mean — I could hardly have come to your house, could I?

TRACEY Flat. We live down the flats. No. My mum's . . . Well, she's not exactly . . . Well, you know.

MISS SMITH The girls in the sixth form told me where you worked. The ones who stayed on.

TRACEY Yeah. The lucky ones.

MISS SMITH You could have done, you know. You got good grades.

TRACEY *almost sarcastically* Oh yes. That would've been brilliant, wouldn't it? Another two years before I started earning.

MISS SMITH *embarrassed* Well. Yes, I see what you mean. I only meant . . .

Pause. **Tracey** *changes the subject, briskly.*

TRACEY No use crying over spilt milk, anyway. And now our Kevin's in trouble again, is he? I just knew it, when you came into the shop. I just knew it.

MISS SMITH He's not in trouble, exactly. I mean — nothing's definite. But . . .

TRACEY But five quid's gone and Kevin was knocking off his lessons. And you think——

MISS SMITH *interrupting* Tracey, I don't necessarily think anything. But it's not as easy as that. Mr Butler's got a sniff of it, and Kevin should have been in Mr Butler's lesson. Mr Butler's . . . well, not to put too fine a point on it, Mr Butler would make a meal of it.

TRACEY He's a pig. He's got no right to be a teacher. He's a pig.

*Pause. **Miss Smith** does not reply, but she clearly doesn't disagree too much.*

TRACEY I didn't think Kevin was nicking any more. That's the really bad thing. I thought he'd given up.

Pause

MISS SMITH We have no evidence that he did. But with Mr Butler . . And anyway . . . I mean, if he *is*. Well, wouldn't it be better if we . . .

TRACEY Nipped it in the bud? *Ironic smile* Sounds easy, doesn't it? Just like that! But . . . what are we going to do?

***Miss Smith** plays with a tea cup.*

MISS SMITH I can't really give advice, of course. But, well, I think you ought to talk to him. Ask him if he did it. Find out.

TRACEY If I can. *Musing* It's our Mum's birthday next week. Maybe that was it.

MISS SMITH I'm sorry?

TRACEY He gets no pocket money, does he? He gets nothing. *Brief pause* He tries to help Mum. He tries to make things nice. *Brief pause* You know. With Dad an' all. I dunno. It's just a thought.

Pause

MISS SMITH Yes.

Pause

TRACEY Well, that's it then, I suppose. I'd better go. He should be home by now.

MISS SMITH What will you do? If he admits it?

TRACEY Oh, I don't suppose he'll admit it. Not just like that, do us a favour. But we understand each other. We'll work something out.

MISS SMITH He can bring it back, of course. I mean, as long as it's returned, it won't be taken any further. Nothing will happen, tell him.

TRACEY You seem to be assuming——

MISS SMITH   I'm not assuming anything. But he ought to talk to me, either way, didn't he? He ought to be warned, if nothing else. About Mr . . . you know.

TRACEY   If he did take it, he'll probably put it in your cubby-hole. In an envelope. Will that do?

MISS SMITH   Absolutely. But . . . but I'd still like to talk to him. Afterwards.

TRACEY   Yeah. Well . . . well, I'll tell him. Keep an eye out, in the morning. But . . . well, I wouldn't sort of come on too heavy, if you know what I mean. Play it careful, like.

Miss Smith laughs

MISS SMITH   Tracey, that is very good advice. I'll be as subtle as a snake.

TRACEY   Yeah. Well, keep an eye out, then. In the morning.

SCENE EIGHT

The playground. A lot of children milling about, dressed against the cold. *Jenny and Buzz in foreground.*

JENNY   I just wonder where he's got to this time, that's all. He'll get in terrible trouble one day. Terrible.

BUZZ   Oh well, at least it runs in the family. He should be used to it.

JENNY   You're horrible, you are. Maybe he's sick.

BUZZ   He's sick all right. In the head. His Dad's a deep-sea diver and there's treasure in the caves. He's nuts. Oy-oy. Is she after us?

He has spotted Miss Smith coming through the crowd. She is obviously looking for someone, and is approaching them.

JENNY   I don't see why she should be. She doesn't even take Kevin, does she?

BUZZ   Kevin? What's it got to do with Kevin?

Miss Smith has arrived. She smiles tentatively.

MISS SMITH   Hello, Jenny. Look — you haven't seen Kevin, have you? Kevin Pelham? He's your friend, isn't he?

JENNY   *to Buzz*   See, stupid. I'm psychic. *To Miss Smith*   No, Miss. Not since last night. I think he's absent.

BUZZ   *sarcastically*   Oh, clever! Take the school prize for logic.

MISS SMITH   Sorry?

JENNY   Don't mind Buzz, Miss. He's an animal. I don't think Kevin's here.

MISS SMITH   But you would have seen him? If he'd turned up today?

JENNY   Well . . . well, he doesn't do the same lessons all the time. He could be . . .

BUZZ   *interrupting*   He could be in the lavs, Miss. He spends a lot of time in there. Or in the caverns.

JENNY   *glaring*   Just shut it.

MISS SMITH   The caverns? I don't quite understand. What——

JENNY   *quickly*   He don't mean nothing, Miss. He's being stupid. It's just our name for . . . for part of the school.

BUZZ   Yeah, it's . . . it's . . . You know. A joke.

She questions him with a look, but gets nowhere. To Miss Smith, though, it doesn't seem important. She wants Kevin.

MISS SMITH   But you haven't seen him anyway. Jenny?

JENNY   No, Miss. Sorry.

Miss Smith is undecided.

MISS SMITH   Ah well.   *She starts to leave. Then stops*   Look . . . last night. You said you spoke to him. Did he . . . was he . . . oh, never mind. Forget it.

JENNY   Miss?

But Miss Smith is leaving. Buzz calls after her.

BUZZ   Shall we tell him, then? If we see him? Do you want to talk to him?

She walks off.

BUZZ If *I* did that, I'd get detention for bad manners . . .

JENNY I wonder where he is . . .

SCENE NINE

*The 'treasure' chamber in the caverns. It is very dark, and at first, silent, but for a steady drip of water. After a short while we hear **Kevin**, some way off. He is shouting.*

KEVIN *off* It's not fair! It's not fair!

He is doing it for the echo, which follows faintly.

ECHO It's not fair . . .

Pause

KEVIN *off* I didn't steal it! I didn't steal it!

ECHO Didn't steal it . . .

Pause

KEVIN *off* One day I'll show them! One day I'll show them!

ECHO One day I'll show them . . .

*After a moment, at some distance, we see the beam of a small, cheap torch. It may disappear, as **Kevin** turns a tunnel corner, then reappear closer. Shortly, **Kevin** reaches the chamber.*

KEVIN *no echo expected now. He is talking to himself, in a flat, fed-up voice* My own sister. Calling me a liar. Well I didn't——

He breaks off. He has seen a blanket in the centre of the chamber. There may be old junk about as well — broken chairs, tables, planks, etc.

KEVIN What's that? A blanket? No one's slept *(down here, surely?)* Hang about!

He goes to the blanket and gingerly pulls it aside. We see a pile of car radios, a couple of small cashboxes, etc.

KEVIN It's radios. *Pause* It's loot. *Pause* It's buried rotten treasure!

14

He picks up a radio and holds it in both hands, wonderingly.

KEVIN At *last!*

SCENE TEN

Paddy's Market, a small, cluttered junk shop. Among the items on view for sale are car radios. The door buzzes and **Kevin** *enters, in his anorak. He pulls out the radio as he approaches* **Paddy,** *a middle-aged man, who eyes him suspiciously.*

PADDY Yes? Can I help you?

KEVIN Oh. Yeah. I . . . I've got this radio. To sell. Do you . . . buy radios?

Paddy takes the set and looks at it.

PADDY I buy radios. Where you get it?

KEVIN It's dead cheap. I mean . . . well, you can have it for a fiver.

PADDY *turning it over* German. Not bad. Five pounds very reasonable.

KEVIN *jokily* Well — it's not much use to me now, is it? Without the car!

PADDY That's right. And what did you say happened? To the car?

KEVIN *slightly flustered* It was nicked. We live down the flats.

PADDY Nick the car and leave the radio. Funny that.

KEVIN Well . . . it was more sort of scrapped, really. They . . . my Dad . . . well, my Dad's buying a new one.

PADDY And you thief your Daddy's radio?

KEVIN No! My Dad's away! He's in Saudi, on the oil rigs. He's a diver.

PADDY So how you get the set?

KEVIN Look — give it back! I don't want to sell it here! Just give it over!

Paddy *holds the radio out of* **Kevin's** *reach. He looks serious.*

15

PADDY   Listen, friend, you don't want to land in trouble, do you? School uniform. Nice tie on. Handling stolen goods a serious offence.

KEVIN   I didn't steal it!

PADDY   Car radios grow on trees round here.   *Brief pause*   So you found it. Still against the law to take it, boy. Stealing by finding. You never hear of that?

KEVIN   Give it to me! *You're* stealing it now! Give it to me!

Paddy sighs. He hands the radio back.

PADDY   See sense. Throw it away if you can't take it back. Throw it away and get into your school. I ain't telling on you.

Kevin goes to the door. He is crushed. He opens it, and speaks over his shoulder, trying for defiance.

KEVIN   My father gave it to me. For some extra pocket money. You're a . . . you're *stupid*.

*The door slams, **Paddy** shakes his head pensively.*

PADDY   *to himself*   And you end up in trouble, Sonny Jim . . .

SCENE ELEVEN

*A street near the school. **Jenny** and **Buzz**, among other kids, are going home.*

JENNY   Maybe he's sick. Maybe we should go round the flats and look for him.

BUZZ   I hate them flats. Stairs!

JENNY   We could use the lift. If it's working.

BUZZ   If you can stand the smell of public lavs. Anyway, I hate his Mum an'all.

JENNY   You're rotten, you are. What's up with his Mum?

BUZZ   How should I know? Maybe she's mad, too. Maybe——

*Suddenly, **Kevin** dives on **Buzz**, from out of a doorway or alleyway. He almost knocks him over.*

KEVIN   Shazzam!

BUZZ   You lunatic! Get off!

JENNY   Where've you *been*?

Kevin brandishes a five pound note.

KEVIN   Never you mind. But it's been *great*.

Miss Smith's voice is heard, off.

MISS SMITH   Kevin! Kevin Pelham!

They look, frozen in shock.

KEVIN   Oh no!

BUZZ   She's after you. She's been after you all day.

Kevin starts to run, but the others hang back.

KEVIN   Down here!   *He stops*   Come on! I've got to show you something.

MISS SMITH   *off, but closer*   Kevin Pelham!

KEVIN   I've got cash. Come *on*.

*He runs off. **Buzz** suddenly follows. **Jenny** hangs back.*

BUZZ   Come on, Jen. Run!

JENNY   *to herself*   We know you've got cash, Kev. Now. It's obvious, isn't it?

MISS SMITH   *off, close*   Jenny!   Jenny!   Come here!

Jenny looks off, and makes up her mind.

JENNY   *to herself*   Sorry, Miss Smith. Sorry.

She races off.

MISS SMITH   *off*   Jennifer!!

SCENE TWELVE

*A shop. **Tracey** is behind the counter, in white coat. **Miss Smith** facing her, in outdoor clothes.*

MISS SMITH   I'm sorry, Tracey, but it does seem to confirm it. He met Jenny and that boy after school and they ran away from me. I imagine he'd spent the day spending my five pounds.

TRACEY *a little bitter* Would it take that long? I— No, I'm sorry. Joke. So now I suppose you call the police?

MISS SMITH *shocked* The police? No, I— Well, I certainly don't think so. Perhaps I'll tell the head and . . . *Pause* I'm so sorry he didn't turn up to talk to me.

TRACEY *grimly* Not as sorry as I am, Miss Smith. He promised me, the little . . .

MISS SMITH Yes.

TRACEY But if you do tell the headteacher . . . Well, won't she call in the police? I mean . . .

Pause

MISS SMITH Look. It's Friday night. At least nothing will happen till Monday, will it? Either way.

TRACEY And on Monday morning . . .

MISS SMITH Tracey. It's two whole days. From my end, nothing will happen till then. OK?

TRACEY I'm not meaning to be rude, honest. It's just . . . I'm sorry.

MISS SMITH That's all right, I understand. I'll leave you to it, then.

She turns to go

TRACEY Yeah, I . . .

MISS SMITH *remembering* Oh Tracey. There was just one thing. Does the word— Do "the caverns" mean anything to you?

*They do, but **Tracey** does not give it away.*

TRACEY Caverns? No, I don't think so. Why?

MISS SMITH Oh nothing. It was probably a joke. That boy mentioned them, that's all. Buzz, does he call himself?

TRACEY Yeah, Buzz. Yes, he's a bit like that. It was probably just a joke. Cheerio, then.

MISS SMITH Bye. Have a nice weekend.

She goes.

TRACEY *to herself, sarcastically* Oh definitely. It's the caverns now, is it? Oh, definitely . . .

SCENE THIRTEEN

The caverns. The kids are around the loot. The blanket has been hauled aside.

BUZZ   Kevin, it's fantastic. It must be worth hundreds. It's incredible.

KEVIN   Thousands, maybe. Well — hundreds, yeah. *Brief pause* Jenny?

JENNY   *sullenly* What?

KEVIN   Aren't we going to say a dicky-bird, then? Are we suffering from total sour grapes?

Buzz has picked up a cashbox. He is hitting it with a brick.

JENNY   What d'you expect me to say? Well done?

KEVIN   Sorry would be a start, wouldn't it? You're just like my ruddy sister, aren't you? Thinking I'd been nicking from a teacher. And you're meant to be my mate.

BUZZ   We could get a hacksaw, maybe. My brother's got one in his car.

JENNY   You can't really blame me, Kev. There's been rumours in the school all day. Someone's stolen something, and you're not there. Then Miss Smith starts acting daft. She's after you. What did you expect me to think?

KEVIN   She's a teacher. Teachers are cracked.

JENNY   Yeah, well she's not that cracked. I'd've been a lot crackeder to believe your precious treasure would turn up, wouldn't I?

BUZZ   It did though, didn't it? Nice one, Kev!

KEVIN   Yeah, it did. And I took a radio and flogged it down Stone Street for a fiver. A big fat woman in a junk shop. No questions asked.

BUZZ   Your trouble is, you've got no faith, Jen. You've got a suspicious mind.

JENNY   Oh don't you start. You thought Kev had nicked it, too. Don't deny it.

KEVIN   Well you're both wrong. I gave up nicking ages ago, I told you. It's a mug's game.

BUZZ   Yeah, and you're . . . *(a mug.)*

He stops. **Kevin** *looks at him, invitingly.*

KEVIN   Go on, Buzz. You were saying . . .?

BUZZ   Look, anyway. Why don't we cut all this arguing? It's a waste of time. We're going to need tools to open up the cashboxes, I reckon.   *He shakes it madly*   So near and yet so far! We could be *rich.*

KEVIN   We'll have to take it out with us.   *Brief pause*   Your Dad's got a workshop hasn't he, Jenny?

JENNY   You must be joking, mate. He'd kill me, wouldn't he?

BUZZ   *genuinely surprised*   What? Why?

JENNY   Because it's stolen goods, you fool. Isn't it?

BUZZ   But *we* didn't steal it!

JENNY   But someone did. So me Dad would go insane. And so would yours.

BUZZ   Kevin? What do you say? *I* reckon——

Suddenly there's a noise, echoing and eerie. Although neither we nor the children know it, it is **Tracey***, calling from one of the caverns' far entrances. Very ghostly.*

TRACEY   *off*   Keeeeeev. Keeeeeev.

The children are transfixed.

JENNY   What is it!

BUZZ   It's coming down here! It's coming to get us! Kev!

TRACEY   *off*   Keeeeev. Keveeeeeee.

Pause. They look at him.

KEVIN   I'm getting out of here.

After a brief pause, they stampede for the exit and disappear. **Buzz** *has picked up his rucksack, though, with a couple of radios in it. When they have gone,* **Tracey** *emerges from the shadows. She is outside the caverns, looking through an entrance hole.*

TRACEY   *starts to shout, then stops*   Ke . . .   *She shakes herself, impatiently*   Oh, what's the flaming use?

She turns and walks away.

SCENE FOURTEEN

*A road outside a department store window. **Buzz** and **Kevin** are jovial. They do not notice **Jenny's** more sombre mood.*

KEVIN   So I thought it was a ghost! So what? If I'd known it was our Tracey I'd've been even scareder!

BUZZ   What d'you think she wanted, though? Skulking around the caves like that.

KEVIN   It sounded really weird. She could've given us all heart attacks.

BUZZ   How did she know, though?

KEVIN   She's always known. Longer than me, even. Dad used to take us down, for laughs. He used to take us on some dead good expeditions.

BUZZ   But how did she know today? That we were down there?

KEVIN   Maybe she just spotted us. Maybe she just followed. Tomorrow's Saturday, though. I'll find out where she's going to be so we can shift the loot in peace.

Buzz holds up the radios and rucksack, triumphantly.

BUZZ   The rest of the loot! I can't wait. Curse my Auntie Doreen coming. I want to do it first thing.

KEVIN   Afternoon job. I've got errands in the morning, anyway. Time and place agreed, right? Look, let's go and flog these two, eh? I'm going to get some scent with my share.

BUZZ   Scent! Have you gone funny?

KEVIN   It's my Mum's birthday. Next Wednesday. Jen? What sort's best? What about that bottle there? Toilet water.

JENNY   *morosely*   How should I know?

KEVIN   You're a girl, aren't you? I just thought . . .

BUZZ   You're raving. The only toilet water Jen'd put behind her ears is——

Jenny thumps him.

JENNY   Don't be filthy, you.

Buzz runs, laughing.

KEVIN   It's dear though, isn't it? I want to buy her something nice.

BUZZ   How much will we get? For these two?

KEVIN   I told you. Fiver each. She said she'd take as many as I could get.

BUZZ   Gaw! Ten whole quid! I'm going to get an Army torch. Two-hundred-metre beam. Come on — let's get shifting. Where's the shop?

*He and **Kevin** begin to move. But **Jenny** hangs back.*

KEVIN   Stone Street. Behind the market. Come on, Jenny.

Pause

JENNY   Kev?

He knows something is wrong.

KEVIN   Yeah?

JENNY   I don't want a share.

KEVIN   You what! You're joking!

BUZZ   Flipping heck, Jenny! Have you gone cracked?

She shrugs, embarrassed.

JENNY   It's just . . . Look — you have mine. Put it towards the scent. I'm going home.

KEVIN   But what . . .? I mean . . .?

*They're all embarrassed. **Jenny** starts to drift away.*

JENNY   I'll see you tomorrow, then. After dinner. Time and place agreed. Right?

They do not reply.

JENNY   *low noise*   Mm.

She goes.

SCENE FIFTEEN

***Kevin's** bedroom. He is still in his anorak, and **Tracey** is confronting him. Voices raised.*

TRACEY Kevin, do you think I'm soft in the head, or something? I *know* you're telling lies. I've spoken to Miss Smith again. Not only did you skip the day at school, not only did you break your promise to talk to her, but you went off with Buzz and Jenny. She saw you!

KEVIN So? That still doesn't mean I stole her money, does it? What about those two? Are they meant to have nicked it too? Eh?

TRACEY I haven't got the foggiest idea. I'm not interested. I'm interested in *you*. Oh Kevin. Don't you understand? You'll end up like your father, that's what I'm scared of. You'll end up in some rotten jail.

Kevin is always crushed by the thought of his lost father. He sits, embarrassed and confused.

KEVIN *muttering* He was framed up, wasn't he? It wasn't his fault. He stole to help the poor.

Tracey is completely amazed by this.

TRACEY *quietly* You what? What did you say? Dad stole to help the poor? *What* poor?!

Put on the spot, Kevin goes for defiance.

KEVIN Us! You and me and Mum! We're poor, aren't we? Aren't we? I don't even get any pocket money, do I? Mum hasn't got a proper coat!

Even to him it sounds ridiculous. He hunches down to hide his shame. Tracey stares at him. She's moved. She sits beside him and tries to touch him, but he draws away.

TRACEY *kindly and carefully* Oh love. Oh Kevvie. Of course we're poor. We are poor. But . . . but Dad isn't Robin Hood. Believe me. Our Dad . . . our Dad's a stupid thief.

Kevin launches himself at her, to try and pummel her. She grabs his wrists to stop him.

KEVIN He's not! He's not! You just don't like him any more! You can't say that about our Dad!

Pause. He struggles, but she is stronger. He subsides.

TRACEY I do like him, Kevin. I love him. But you've got to face it. He's a thief. A burglar. And you're not going to end up like him, not if I can help it. You're just not.

Pause. He lets her put her arm around his shoulders.

KEVIN *hopelessly* I never stole that money from the school, Trace. If only you'd believe me. I've not nicked *anything*.

Pause. **Tracey** *gazes forward.*

TRACEY I don't know what to say, our kid. That's the problem. You see, your Dad does this to Mum. To me and Mum. Every time. Any time something happens, he swears it wasn't him. He swears black's white he's going straight, he's learnt his lesson. *Brief pause* And we believe him. *Brief pause* And then the knock comes. On the door. And he's arrested. That's why Mum cries, Kev. She cries herself to sleep. We've seen it all before.

A long pause.

KEVIN *quietly* But I've not nicked anything, Tracey. I haven't. You should believe me.

Tracey *stands up.*

TRACEY I'm not saying any more. I don't dare to. No more questions, no more truth, no more lies. Whatever. If you did take something, give it back. All right?

KEVIN I didn't, though. Honestly.

TRACEY *watching him closely* And those old caverns. Miss Smith thought you'd gone off there. I went down looking for you.

Kevin *is shaken, but he does not look at her.* *Pause.*

KEVIN *quietly* They're all bricked up. The council's always down there.

TRACEY They're dangerous. I'm not asking if you play there because I'm scared of hearing lies. But if you have been — don't. I'm telling you not to. For all our sakes. Right?

She tries to make him look at her, but he will not.

KEVIN *mutters* The council's bricked them up. They're . . .

TRACEY *stands away.* *She thinks he's lying.*

TRACEY *coldly* Just think about it, eh? And what it's doing to our Mum. Just think about it.

She is leaving.

KEVIN *quietly* Yeah.

*When **Tracey** has gone, he stands up. After a pause, he slowly takes out a big bottle of toilet water. He looks at it for a moment or two, troubled. Then, rapidly, he hides it.*

KEVIN *to himself* Yeah.

SCENE SIXTEEN

***Kevin, Jenny** and **Buzz** in the woods above the caves. All in anoraks, **Jenny** in jeans, not skirt. She is carrying an entrenching tool or small shovel.*

BUZZ *angrily* It's ridiculous, that's why! *Might* get a reward! *Might* get a few quid! You're chickening out, that's the real truth!

JENNY I am not chickening out. I'm here, aren't I? I borrowed my brother's Army shovel-thing.

BUZZ You're here, but you might as well not be. We thought you weren't coming, didn't we, Kev? We had bets on it.

JENNY And I did. So you're wrong. I'm telling you, Buzz, this plan's sense. This way we might actually get some money.

BUZZ Get told to take a running jump, more like. I'm telling you, Jen, if we go to the police, we'll get arrested.

JENNY Why should we? We've found some stuff in the caverns, right? Some stolen stuff. And we report it. They'll be grateful.

BUZZ *short laugh* You've been reading too many kids' books, you have. Emily and the Detectives. Defectives, more like!

JENNY You're the defective. You've got no brains at all. If we move the stuff, if we sell it, if we touch it, even, probably — we've broken the law. So we bury it! We tell the cops! Kevin — what do you think?

KEVIN Well. . .

BUZZ Yeah, you tell her, Kev! Tell her she's raving! Tell her she's a rotten little coward! Go on.

Pause.

KEVIN   Let's go down.

JENNY   Yeah!

BUZZ   Why, though? What to do? Flog the stuff? Or ruddy bury it?

KEVIN   *leading the way*   We'll go to the rope entrance. We can drop down. It's near the treasure cave.

BUZZ   Kevin! Are you chickening out as well? Kev!

*He is trying to stop **Kevin** going, to get an answer. But **Kevin** moves on doggedly. They are almost off.*

KEVIN   Buzz, I . . . I think she's right.

BUZZ   But you can't! It's mad. *You're* mad.

KEVIN   I really think she's right . . .

*They have gone. But almost immediately, two men come on from another direction. They have obviously been watching the children. They are the thieves, **Bob** and **Alan.***

BOB   I thought they'd never go. Jack'll go insane if we leave him with the van much longer.

ALAN   Jack's insane already. Don't kid yourself.

BOB   You know what I mean. Can you see them?   *(The kids.)*

ALAN   Nah. They'll have gone off playing in the woods. They won't bother us.

BOB   They couldn't get down there, could they? Find the stuff?

ALAN   What are you on about? You're as daft as Jack, you are. They're kids. Messing in the woods.

BOB   Yeah, I suppose you're right. Oh well — we'd better get him.

***Alan** indicates with his head.*

ALAN   Too late. He's here.

***Jack** enters. He is a glowering, thin-faced man, with a menacing air.*

JACK   Are you two trying to be funny? Because if you are . . .

ALAN   We were just coming for you, mate. The coast's clear.

BOB   Let's go down.

SCENE SEVENTEEN

Kevin's bedroom. **Tracey** *is hoovering, and the nozzle has found the bottle of toilet water in its hiding place. She switches off, takes the bottle, and stares at it, puzzled.*

MUM *off* Tracey? Trace?

Tracey *rapidly hides the bottle and flips a duster about.*

MUM *entering* Finished, love? Or had enough?

TRACEY No, I . . . I was just thinking, that's all.

MUM Thinking what? That you do too much for Kevin? He's a mucky little devil. He should learn.

TRACEY No, not that. It's just . . . Oh, I think I need a break, that's all. I'm going for a wander. Anything you need?

MUM That's right, love, you get some fresh air, eh?

TRACEY Yeah. I think I better had.

SCENE EIGHTEEN

The treasure chamber. Pitch black. After a short pause, we see powerful lights, not the children's torches. We hear **Jack** *and* **Alan** *approaching.*

JACK Yeah, well. Bob can sort it out then, can't he? He's no use down here anyway. He's clumsy.

ALAN He's crash hot with the van *Of the cave* In here.

The lights come full into the chamber. They flash all over the place, picking out the blanket.

JACK Alan! It's been shifted!

ALAN It can't have been!

JACK Someone's been here! The gear's all over the place. Look!

They pull the blanket. The loot is spread about.

JACK There's radios gone! Some crafty— Who the hell——

ALAN *doubtfully* It could be kids.

JACK *scornful* Kids my— *Pause. Suspicious* Why kids? Why did you say kids?

ALAN Nah, you're probably right. We spotted some, that's all. Up top. Hanging around. We thought they'd gone away.

JACK And you think— Well I'm telling you. If they're down here——

ALAN Calm down, Jack. They were only kids, if it was them. I mean.

JACK I don't care who it was! If they see us! If they tell the law!

ALAN For God's sake, Jack! Cool it, mate! There's no harm done. Half a dozen radios.

JACK That's not the point! If——

ALAN If you keep shouting——

JACK *hisses* Tssssh! Listen! Tsssh!

They listen. **Jack** *reaches across and turns* **Alan's** *light off. Then he snaps his own out.*

ALAN *cautiously* We can't do anything to them. If——

JACK Shut your *mouth*.

Pause.

ALAN *quieter* If it's only kids, Jack——

There is a movement in the darkness. **Jack** *is gripping him.*

JACK Alan. I promise you. Shut . . . up.

In the silence, we hear the children. **Kevin's** *voice is raised in exasperation against* **Buzz.**

KEVIN *off* Of course I've changed my tune, you wally. It's stolen, isn't it? Can't you grasp that fact?

BUZZ *off* But——

KEVIN *off* For cripes sake, Jenny — sing.

As we see their dim torches in the background, **Kevin** *and* **Jenny** *resume a song.*

KIDS Hi ho, hi ho, it's off to work we go, Hi ho hiho, hi ho hiho, hi ho, hi ho!

*As they enter, **Jack** turns his light on, blinding them.*

JACK *furiously* I'll give you stolen! I'll murder you!

*As he plunges forward, **Alan** grabs at him and is thrown off. The children scream.*

ALAN Jack! It's *children!*
KEVIN Run!

*They do, with **Jack** blundering after them and tripping over piled junk. The children vanish.*

JACK Get Bob down! You prat, call Bob! We'll have them! Like rats in a trap!
ALAN Jack, they're children.
JACK Call Bob.

SCENE NINETEEN

*In another part of the caverns, in the dark, the **children** appear. They have only one torch now, and it is very dim. From afar, **Alan** can be heard calling for **Bob**.*

BUZZ Who's Bob when he's out? It's a dog! I bet it's a dog!

*There is a note of panic in his voice, which **Jenny** treats irritably.*

JENNY Shut up, Buzz. Keep the noise down.
BUZZ You should've brought your map, Kev. We're lost.
KEVIN No we're not. We're near the bomb store. The one I told you about. Once we get through the bomb door we're safe.
JENNY How do you mean, safe? Is there a way out? Into the woods?
KEVIN Yeah, I . . . Well, it doesn't matter, does it? Because they'll never find it, anyway. I'm the only one that knows it. We'll hide in there until they've gone. We're safe.
BUZZ But what if they know it, too? What if——
KEVIN Buzz, I'm telling you. You're a pain, you are. You've done nothing but whine. You're a pain.

JENNY   But if they do know the door——

KEVIN   Don't you start! One's enough! Look, it's down here! Look, there's the doors.

BUZZ   Kevin. I've lost my torch.

MEN   *off, loud*   Hey! You kids! Come out! Come out!

BUZZ   Oh my G——

JACK   *off*   We're coming to get you.

Pause

KEVIN   *shakily*   It's just down here. Come on . . .

*Cut to blackout. After a pause, there is a huge metallic bang, which reverberates. Then silence. Then, still in blackout, we hear **Jack's** voice, low and penetrating.*

JACK   Done. No way out. Like rats in a big steel trap.

The three men's torches snap on simultaneously, and they walk silently in file across the floor and out.

SCENE TWENTY

*Miss Smith's house. **Miss Smith** and **Tracey** are sitting talking. Tea cups.*

MISS SMITH   *getting at her*   I wish you'd told me about the caverns earlier, Tracey. When I asked. It might have helped, you know.

*She does not say how, but **Tracey** is too subdued to argue.*

TRACEY   I know. I'm sorry. But if you're going to get at me——

MISS SMITH   *realising she's doing it*   No. No of course not.   *Flash of humour*   I'm not your teacher now, am I?

TRACEY   I'm still not certain, that's the trouble. I went down there and saw this bloke, but he said he was from the council.

MISS SMITH   Yes. Difficult.   *Brief pause*   Did he *look* like a council workman?

TRACEY   I don't know. Yes, probably. But the van was a bit old. You know. Knackered.

MISS SMITH   Did you take its number?

*Pause. **Tracey** realises she's been stupid.*

TRACEY   No.

Pause

MISS SMITH   Never mind.   *Pause*   Look, Tracey, quite honestly, I think you're probably worrying too much. It's probably nothing. But if you *are* worried — well, why not call the police?

TRACEY   *quickly*   No!

Miss Smith, *who does not have the Pelham family's fear/ attitude, does not really understand.*

MISS SMITH   But why not? It seems obvious to me. Logical.

*Pause. **Tracey** searches for a convincing reason.*

TRACEY   There's so much hassle, isn't there? I mean — your five pound note, like. He did — well, I found a bottle of toilet water. In his room.

MISS SMITH   Toilet water! Kevin!

*It's a brave attempt at a joke, but **Tracey** does not respond.*

TRACEY   I told you. Mum's birthday. I'm pretty sure he must've stolen your cash for that.   *Brief pause*   He does try.

Pause

MISS SMITH   Yes. I'm sorry. But Tracey — for heaven's sake, love. You don't think I'd call the police in for a fiver, do you? I wouldn't *mention* it if you want to ring them. It's forgotten.

TRACEY   *a touch bitterly*   Until Monday.

MISS SMITH   *on the spot*   Well . . . well, it will have to be sorted out, won't it? But — Tracey, call the police.

Tracey *stands up.*

TRACEY   I think I'd better go now. Thanks for the tea. I'll . . . I'll go and have another look, maybe. Mum will be worrying.

MISS SMITH   *standing*   But surely. I mean, if they *are* in the caves and the police found them. Well, they'd only get a ticking off, wouldn't they? They'd be safe, at least.

TRACEY Yeah. I . . . Look, I'd better go.

MISS SMITH You can ring from here.

Tracey is near the door.

TRACEY I'll think about it. I . . .

Miss Smith tries a small bright laugh, which sounds false.

MISS SMITH Don't you believe in justice, then? The police?

TRACEY *going* Mum'll be worrying.

Miss Smith stands alone, pondering. She knows **Tracey** *will not phone.*

SCENE TWENTY-ONE

A dark tunnel. The **children** *are huddled at one end, with a glimmer of light coming through a ventilator hole that has been blocked up from outside. They have been there for ages, and they are exhausted. No one speaks for some time.*

JENNY It's getting dark outside. Do you think they'll find us soon? It's getting dark.

Pause

KEVIN It's not that cold though, is it? *Brief pause* They must've missed us by now, they must've.

BUZZ *he's angry and afraid* Why? Why must they? Why should anybody miss us?

JENNY Ssh. Buzz. Don't act daft, we'll be all right.

KEVIN Honest, Buzz. My sister knows about the caves. She'll——

BUZZ Your sister's as daft as you are! She's a thickie just like you! Just like all the Pelham family! You got us into this, Kevin. You're stupid, stupid!

Pause

KEVIN I knew there was a ventilator hole down here. I didn't know they'd blocked it up, that's all.

BUZZ *loses his anger, but only to be depressed* That's all, is it? Isn't that fantastic. You knew there was a ventilator but you didn't know it was blocked up, that's all. Just like knowing it was safe to come in through the bomb doors until someone closed them on us and chucked away the key. Isn't that fantastic.

KEVIN *also depressed* If we'd stayed out in the passages——

BUZZ *interrupting* Why don't you just shut up, eh? Give your brain a rest. It's like everything else about you, Kevin Pelham. Useless. If *you* say we'll be all right, I bet we die. I *bet*.

Pause. **Buzz** *starts to sniff, quite loudly.* **Jenny** *tries to comfort him.*

JENNY *kindly* Try not to cry, Buzz. It doesn't help. If——

BUZZ *strangled* I'm not crying, stupid! I'm *cold*.

JENNY Oh.

Pause. With a click, **Kevin** *turns the torch on.*

KEVIN Maybe there's enough to signal with. Maybe if . . .

The torch glows for a moment or two, then fades. The light from the ventilator is dimmer as well.

JENNY *so that* **Buzz** *won't hear* Do you really think they'll rescue us, Kev? Soon? I'm cold, too. I'm freezing.

Pause

KEVIN We'd better shout again. Maybe someone's in the woods. A courting couple, maybe.

JENNY In winter?

KEVIN What else can we do?

Fade to blackout. Then we hear **Miss Smith**, *either in total darkness, amplified, or with her picked out in a spotlight, alone. She is on the telephone.*

MISS SMITH Police? Yes, my name's Judith Smith. Yes, look. I understand there are some caves or something, under Vintners Wood. Yes. Well . . . well, I have reason to believe . . .

Fade to silence and blackout.

SCENE TWENTY-TWO

*The woods. Dusk. **Tracey's** voice is heard, off. Excited. She has heard them shouting.*

TRACEY *shouting* But where, Kevin, where? It's me! It's Tracey!

***Kevin** and **Jenny** are heard, off.*

KEVIN Over here! Tracey! Here!

JENNY There's a pile of rocks! Concrete!

KEVIN We're over here!

*Fade light to black, then bring up to dusk. **Tracey** is scrabbling at the rubble outside the blocked-up ventilator. Surprisingly, **Kevin** sounds excited and full of life. Now he's found, he assumes all his troubles are over.*

KEVIN *out of view, or just visible* It's brilliant! Brilliant! We've found some loot! We'll tell the police! Cash boxes!

***Tracey** can hardly surpress her anger.*

TRACEY Just shut up and help. You fool!

KEVIN But we're heroes! They tried to kill us! Men!

*As he says it, and as **Tracey's** attitude sinks in, he becomes less certain.*

KEVIN If anything . . . If anything, we're heroes . . .

Bring up, loud, a blaring police siren. Hold for several seconds, then silence.

KEVIN *uncertainly* Trace . . .

TRACEY *furiously* Oh shut your stupid *mouth.*

As she tears spasmodically at the rubble, torches begin to flash, hurrying towards them.

POLICE *off* Police! Where are you? We're on our way.

TRACEY *wearily* This time, Kev, you've done it properly. This time — you're in trouble.

SCENE TWENTY-THREE

The kitchen in Kevin's flat. **Mum**, *looking drained and ill, is sitting.* **Kevin**, *clean and polished in different clothes, is pressed into a chair, trying to be invisible. It is next morning.*

KEVIN Why are they taking so long? Why won't she let them in?

MUM *listlessly* It's not a good idea to make them stand outside. It might provoke them.

KEVIN *Can* they come in? If they want to? Can they arrest me?

MUM They can do anything they like. She should let them in. She should know better.

KEVIN But they couldn't take me away, could they? You wouldn't let them, would you? Not take me away?

The door opens and **Kevin** *flinches. But only* **Tracey** *comes in. She looks grim.* **Kevin** *presses himself further into his seat.*

MUM Have they gone?

TRACEY Yes. For the moment. I told them he was a kid. I told them they could talk to him when they'd made their minds up.

KEVIN *fearfully* About what? I talked to them last night. I told them everything.

MUM Are they going to prosecute?

TRACEY That's what I said. They don't know yet. That's what I'm *telling* you.

KEVIN Tracey, you believe me, don't you? Now. I'm *not* a little liar any more. I'm not a thief.

Tracey looks at him without replying. Then she goes to the sideboard or a cupboard. When she turns back, she is holding the bottle of toilet water. **Kevin** *is shocked.*

TRACEY *flatly* What's this, then? Scotch mist?

Kevin's voice is almost inaudible.

KEVIN It's my birthday present. For our Mum. Scent.

Mum *looks at it. She does not seem able to take it in.*

MUM   *listlessly*   Oh, Kevin.

TRACEY   *harshly*   It's stolen property, isn't it? From Miss Smith's five pound note.

KEVIN   *passionately*   No! From the radios! I told you, I don't nick no more. The radios!

Tracey is surprised. But she believes him.

TRACEY   Oh.   *She half smiles, pleased. Then she remembers*   Still stolen property, though, isn't it?   *Brief pause*   Sorry.

KEVIN   *dully*   But we knew. We'd worked it out, me and Jenny. We were going to get the reward, then buy back the three that we'd flogged. We were going to give them in as well. We thought we might be heroes.

Tracey smiles ruefully. She puts the bottle on the table.

TRACEY   *gently*   You still believe in Robin Hood, don't you, our kid? But there aren't any heroes. There won't be a reward . . . The police checked the caves and there's nothing there. I saw the van and I didn't even get the number. Heroes!

Pause

KEVIN   *low*   I wish you'd've believed me when I told you, though. About not nicking from the teacher. I wasn't telling lies.

TRACEY   No. But that's the trouble, isn't it? No one will believe you, will they? And whose fault's that? Jenny's Mum and Dad, Buzz's Mum and Dad, last night. They blamed it all on you, didn't they? You're known for it. The cops'll be back soon enough. You might get prosecuted. I'd probably better even hide that rotten scent. Chuck it down the lavatory.

Pause

KEVIN   I thought they'd all be pleased with me for once. Everyone.   *Brief pause*   Even if I'd gone to the coppers in the first place they wouldn't've believed me, would they? They'd've said I nicked it, or something. I'm like my Dad. They know me. I'm a thief.

Pause

TRACEY Not any more, though, eh? I believe you, Kevvie. That's a start, isn't it?

Pause

KEVIN You didn't, though. Not until . . . I wish you'd've believed me when I said.

Tracey goes towards the door.

TRACEY I'm sorry, love. But I do believe you now. You'll have to make do with that, won't you. It's a start. Mum? Do you want a cup of tea?

She goes. Pause.

MUM You will be all right, though, won't you, Kevin? *Brief pause* Kev?

Pause. They look at the bottle.

KEVIN I wanted you to have a happy birthday, Mum. That's all.

Pause. She looks at him, and nods.

MUM You're very like your father sometimes, Kev.

They look at the bottle of scent.

PERFORMING THE THIEF

The Thief started life as a play for television in four parts. It has been rewritten as a text that can be done in one of a number of ways, with a small or large cast, elaborate or simple staging, in the classroom or on a stage, as it is or improvised around. There is also a novel of *The Thief* in which Jan Needle has changed some of the scenes and characters. You might wish to use some of that. You could experiment with different media and see how this effects the way you act — stage acting usually needs to be 'bigger' than acting for a camera or microphone, even in a naturalistic drama like *The Thief* — and what you require to make the play 'work'. Above all the play is meant to be done in the way that you think best.

THE THIEF AS A FILM

You might decide to do it as it was originally done, as a film, using your own school, homes and streets as locations. If you do not have caves in your area, you could look for a site that could be filmed to look like caves, or make a simple 'set' for the caves — if you look carefully at the scenes in the caverns you will see how they could be suggested by using a blacked-out hall, sound effects and torches. Or there is probably somewhere in your area that, like Kevin's caves, is ancient, dangerous and forbidden territory to children that might be used as a hiding place by thieves — a derelict church, warehouse or old house. *** You could easily adapt the play to fit your circumstances and make it a film about your 'patch'. If your school does not have video or

*** WARNING. If you do use one of these 'forbidden' places, only do so with adult permission and supervision. As Kevin finds out, they are DANGEROUS.

film equipment, you might be able to borrow a 'Camcorder' —
one of the domestic video cameras that are now readily available
— and with careful preparation use that.

Approach

Unless you have elaborate editing equipment that enables you
to shoot the film in any sequence, you will have to film the play in
narrative order. This means that you will need plenty of
organisation. You will have to work out what you want for each
scene in advance — setting, lighting, sound effects, actors' and
camera moves — because you won't be able to go back and do
things again. Where you have two scenes in the same place, like
the caves or Kevin's bedroom, which have to look the same each
time, but which are in different parts of the story, you will have
to take great care that the continuity is right, i.e. that
everything is in exactly the same place. It helps if you can take a
polaroid picture of the set, then you can check the details when
you come to the scene again.

Suggested order for work

1   Make a list of all the scenes. You might choose not to do some
scenes or to alter them. You could use a 'voice-over' narrator for
some scenes or instead of some scenes.

2   Find locations for the scenes. Or work out sets where this is
appropriate.

3   Most video equipment will work in any light conditions, but it
is best to check that you are going to get the effect you want
before you film. Do a trial 'shoot'. You might need some lighting
effects in, say, the caves. While torches in the dark may be very
dramatic, you might require some supplementary lighting in
order to see the children's faces.

4   Work out and record, if necessary, any sound effects that you
may want. Live sound effects usually sound better. Work out
where they should come from in relation to the camera
microphone. In scene thirteen, for example, you wouldn't want
Tracey's voice too close to the children when she follows them to
the cave and calls down to them from above. In other scenes you
could get some exciting dramatic effects with sounds getting

closer — like the children's voices in scene eighteen when they are returning to the cave when the robbers are there. Again, do a trial run.

5 Actors' moves need to be plotted carefully so that the camera can follow them and not suddenly lose a character 'out of shot' because the actor has changed her or his mind about where they are going!

6 The camera is the 'eye' that is going to tell the story. It can tell the story quite simply by standing back and just filming what is in front of it. Or it can enhance the drama by selecting how it tells the story. Take the following example: scene two.

You could set up the camera in front of the line of coats with the figure rooting among them, letting the actions of the actor create the mystery about who he or she is and what they're doing.

Or you could let the camera help:

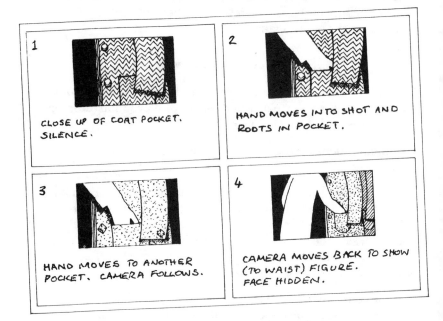

1 CLOSE UP OF COAT POCKET. SILENCE.

2 HAND MOVES IN TO SHOT AND ROOTS IN POCKET.

3 HAND MOVES TO ANOTHER POCKET. CAMERA FOLLOWS.

4 CAMERA MOVES BACK TO SHOW (TO WAIST) FIGURE. FACE HIDDEN.

5

LAVATORY FLUSHES OFF CAMERA.

6

CAMERA MOVES BACK TO SHOW HAND OF THIEF DROP WALLET ON FLOOR.

7

HAND MOVES DOWN TOWARDS WALLET. HESITATES. DRAWS BACK SHARPLY. HAS £5 NOTE IN HAND.

8

CAMERA DRAWS BACK AS THIEF RUNS. WE SEE IT IS NOT KEVIN.

9

CAMERA HOLDS SHOT ON COAT-RACK. SOUND OF DOOR BANGING OFF CAMERA. MR. ATKINSON COMES INTO SHOT *. PICKS UP WALLET.
*"HALLO? WHAT'S GOING ON?"

10

CAMERA FOLLOWS MR. ATKINSON TO DOOR. OPENS DOOR.

11

CAMERA LOOKS DOWN EMPTY CORRIDOR.

12

CUT TO MR. ATKINSON'S HAND. OPENS WALLET.
"JUDY SMITH'S. I WONDER IF ANYTHING'S GONE."

Filming the whole of *The Thief* would be a very big project. You might choose to film just a few scenes. The class could divide into four groups and take a key scene or couple of scenes each. You would still need to think about the details in the same way as you would if you were filming the whole play.

41

THE THIEF AS A RADIO PLAY

You might consider doing the play as a radio play. There are plenty of challenges in the text and scope for imaginative dramatic work in creating the different settings through sound only. How, for example, would you differentiate between the scenes in the school classroom, the cloakroom and the staffroom using just voices and sound effects? How would you create the atmosphere in the caves? It would also give you an opportunity to put back into the play some of the things that were in the original TV play — like the dog chase in the caves — or in the novel, or to invent some scenes of your own.

Approach

Again, your main problem will be one of organisation. If you have access to a reel-to-reel tape recorder then you can approach the play quite freely. You can record in any order, then edit the tape; you can record and dub sounds, and correct any errors easily. If, however, you have a cassette tape recorder that you cannot edit, life is more complicated. As with the Camcorder, you will have to record in narrative order. With a second cassette recorder it is possible to dub. You can record one sound on to one player — for example, the sound of the children running away at the end of scene eighteen — then add it to the dialogue of the thieves as you record that.

The other challenge you will find with turning *The Thief* into a radio play is finding a way to set the scene through sound. Sometimes the words can do it for you. The first scene in Kevin's bedroom is very clearly established by the dialogue between Kevin and Mum as 'at home', and the transistor helps make it clear we are in Kevin's domain. Sometimes the sounds required by the script will set the scene, as in the first scene with the babble of children's voices and the school buzzer sounding. There's no mistaking that! At other times you could add a few words of dialogue yourself to set the scene. Some scenes have very little dialogue and these will require special thought.

Planning and imagination are the keys!

Suggested order for work

1   Decide whether you are going to use a 'framing' device to indicate a change of scene. Music can be very atmospheric. A narrator would help solve the problem of scene setting.

2   Make a list of scenes and decide which need altering because you are only using sound.

3   Take each scene and work out how you are going to do it.

4   Pre-record any sound effects that are going to be dubbed. Experiment with different ways of achieving effects. Think about the dramatic ways in which you can use sound to enhance the tension.

5   Rehearse with effects and actors, checking the balance between the voices and sound effects.

6   Record scene by scene.

Here is a suggestion for a soundscript for scene two:

SCENE TWO

THE STAFF CLOAKROOM. THERE IS A LINE OF COATS ON A HORIZONTAL ①
RAIL, WITH SOMEONE ROOTING AMONG THEM② FROM BEHIND, IT COULD
BE KEVIN - THE SAME MINIMAL SCHOOL UNIFORM OF GREY TROUSERS AND
SHIRT, AND BLUE JUMPER. THE FACE IS HIDDEN IN THE COATS.
   THEN A LAVATORY FLUSHES③ AND THE FIGURE FREEZES④ IT
SCRABBLES WITH SOMETHING IN ITS HANDS, AND A WALLET IS DROPPED
TO THE FLOOR⑤ THE FIGURE STOOPS TO RETRIEVE IT⑥ THINKS AGAIN,
AND TURNS TO RUN. IN ONE HAND IS A BANKNOTE. FULL FACE, WE
SEE THAT IT IS NOT KEVIN. THE THIEF RUNS OUT⑦
   FROM BEHIND, A TEACHER - TIM ATKINSON - EMERGES, LOOKING
PUZZLED.

MR ATKINSON (CALLS) Hallo? ⑧

HE COMES TO THE FRONT OF THE COATRACK AND SEES THE WALLET ON
THE FLOOR. HE PICKS IT UP. ⑨

MR ATKINSON What's going on?

HE MOVES RAPIDLY TO THE DOOR AND LOOKS UP AND DOWN THE
CORRIDOR. ⑩ NOTHING. ⑪ HE FLIPS OPEN THE WALLET AND LOOKS AT THE
NAME AND ADDRESS IN THE CLEAR WINDOW.

MR ATKINSON ⑫ Judy Smith's. I wonder if anything's gone ...

SCENE TWO

① SILENCE

② SOUND OF SOMEONE ROOTING IN POCKETS ACCOMPANIED BY
LOW MUTTERING AS CAMERA MOVES FROM COAT TO COAT –
VERY CLOSE TO MICROPHONE.
"LOOKS LIKE OLD WIGGY'S RAG ... NOTHING ... TYPICAL."
VERY QUIET AND INDISTINCT.

③ LAVATORY FLUSH – AT A DISTANCE.

④ INTAKE OF BREATH BY THE THIEF. STILL CLOSE.

⑤ SOUND OF SCRABBLING AND DROPPING OF WALLET.
EXCLAMATION FROM THIEF "OH NO!"

⑥ THIEF "A FIVER! THAT'LL DO" VOICE SHOULD NOW BE
CLEAR – DEFINITELY NOT KEVIN. POSSIBLY A 'BETTER
CLASS' OF BOY, OR A GIRL.

⑦ SOUND OF FEET RUNNING AWAY AND DOOR BANGING.

⑧ MR. ATKINSON'S VOICE, COMING TOWARDS THE MICROPHONE.

⑨ AT MICROPHONE. MR. ATKINSON "WHAT'S THIS? A WALLET?"

⑩ HEAVIER FEET THAN BEFORE MOVE AWAY. DOOR OPENS.

⑪ MR. ATKINSON: "NOTHING." "NO ONE."

⑫ CLOSER TO MICROPHONE.

44

One way of organising your soundscript is as a 'score'.

	①		②	③
DIALOGUE			"LOOKS LIKE WIGGY'S RAG..." "NOTHING... TYPICAL..."	
SPECIAL SOUND EFFECTS		SCHOOL BELL	SILENCE	LAVATORY FLUSH
BACKGROUND SOUNDS	CHILDREN IN PLAYGROUND (DISTANT)			
TIMING	← 5 SECS →	← 1 SEC →	← 1 SEC → ← 2 SECS →	← 15 SECS → ← 1 SEC →

Again, recording the whole play would require a lot of time, but you could experiment with a couple of scenes or divide into groups and take a sequence of scenes each.

You could use musical signs like:

GETTING LOUDER

GETTING SOFTER

45

THE THIEF ON STAGE

If you want to perform the play on a stage, there is one thing you will have to think about very early on. The play has a lot of different settings and some of the scenes are very short. The play could get very long and tedious if there were scene changes between each scene. *The Thief* is set in the 'real world' — it is about children and adults that you might know — so the settings should suggest this. But this doesn't mean that you have to show the whole of, say, the playground or Kevin's bedroom. It is easy to show where the characters are by choosing a simple representative piece of furniture, prop, costume or sound effect.

Given the number of different settings in the play, a school hall stage is probably the worst place to perform *The Thief*! Though that doesn't mean that you shouldn't use it at all. You could, for example, exploit its height to show Tracey on the surface above the caves in scenes thirteen and twenty-two or use it for more permanent sets like Kevin's bedroom, that are used more than twice, and play the other scenes on the hall floor.

Some suggestions for staging

1   Think about different types of staging and the ways in which you can exploit height and space by using rostra.

2   The audience don't have to sit facing the stage squarely (**a**). They could be either side of the action (**b**) or on three sides (**c**).

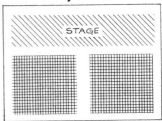

a

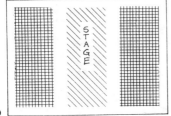

b

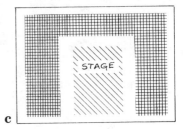

c

The audience could even sit on mats in the middle and the action could go on around them (**d**).

d

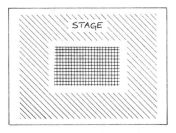

3   Actors don't have to enter straight on to the stage. The aisles can be used. Characters can come from behind the audience.

e

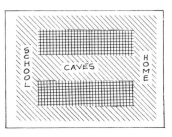

4   Think of scenery that can be used in a number of ways: a coatrack that is just that for the scene in the staff cloakroom, but when turned round is hung with junk for Paddy's shop; a long low table with a bedspread on is Kevin's bed, but with a few cushions is a sofa in Miss Smith's house.

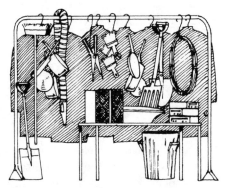

5   Scenes can be created just by using sound effects or lighting. This is particularly true of the scenes in the caves. Imagine what sounds there might be in a cave system, ten or twenty metres underground. How could you convey the eeriness, the chill and sense of danger? Does the cave have an echo, dripping water, bats?

ACTIVITIES ON OR AROUND THE PLAY

Whichever way you choose to tackle *The Thief*, the most important element will be the *acting*. A lot of the play is about Kevin's relationships with other people, his family, friends and figures in authority like teachers and the police. Improvising scenes between characters can help you understand them better and consequently present them in a more complex and truthful fashion in performance.

Many of the exercises and improvisations in this section and in 'Jailbirds' (pages 60–64) will help you fill out details about Kevin's own character and that of his family and friends.

Now you will have to think about ways in which this understanding can be fed into your acting. Here are some suggestions:

1 *Appearances*
a How to picture a character — As we see in 'Jumping to Conclusions' (pages 81–92), we often judge people by the way they look. But people cannot help how they were born — pretty, plain, jug-eared, short, tall, red-headed, big-nosed — and often our experiences and background affect the way we look as well.

Take Kevin, what sort of boy do you think he is physically? Small? Tall? Fat? Thin? Bespectacled? Strong? Fast? Stringy?

Here are some other questions that might help you picture Kevin: with the father often in jail, the Pelham family are quite poor. How does this affect what Kevin wears? Are his clothes like those of the other kids in his class? What effect does this have on Kevin and the way he wears his clothes?

Kevin doesn't get on at school. How does this affect the way he goes to school? Does he run, walk cheerfully, slouch, hang about on corners? How does he behave in class? Where does he sit in the classroom if he gets the choice?

Kevin has a reputation for telling lies or exaggerating. People don't believe Kevin even when he's telling the truth. How does this affect Kevin? Does this influence his manner when he's talking to people? Does he look guilty, even when he's not?

He has a particularly bad relationship with figures in authority — teachers, the police etc. How does this affect the way he behaves towards such people, compared with his behaviour with his friends?

b 'Hot-seating' — A good way to establish these characteristics is to interview intensively or 'hot seat' the character. In groups of five or six, one person playing Kevin, everybody takes turns to question Kevin. The questions can be like those above or delve into other aspects of Kevin's life — his favourite music, food, most happy memory. 'Kevin' can either answer in character or store up the answers in his head as part of his character background. It helps if rather than answering some questions verbally, the actor *shows* the others in the group, e.g. the way in which Kevin walks to school.

This 'hot seating' can then be done with the other characters in the play.

2 *Relationships*

a In the family — Our relationship with each individual member of our family is different, consequently we often tell different versions of the truth to different people. Kevin is just like the rest of us in that respect. Working in groups of four, one person be Kevin, the others, Tracey, his Mum and his Dad. First improvise a scene in which Kevin tells each of them in turn about something that has happened to him that day (perhaps a class with Mr Butler in which he was given detention, or an encounter with some stray dogs on the way home in which his coat got torn). How does he change the story to suit each person? How do they each respond?

Now in the same groups, show how Kevin tells the story of his adventures in the caves to each member of his family.

b Taking after Dad — Kevin's Mum and Tracey both say how like his Dad he is. What sort of things do you imagine Kevin and his father do when Kevin's Dad is not in jail? In the novel of *The Thief* we are told that it was Kevin's father who introduced him to the caves when he was younger. In pairs, improvise the scene in which Kevin and his father first go down the caves.

c   Persuading others — In the novel it is also made clear that, like Kevin, his Dad also had a different perception of the truth than most of the rest of the world. Working in a group of five, imagine a scene in which Kevin brings home a dog he has 'found loose on the common' — a greyhound. Improvise the scene in which he tries to persuade his parents to let him keep the dog.

d   Sharing good times — Good things do happen to Kevin and his family. What do you think they are? In groups of four, improvise one such time, perhaps from when the children were younger.

e   Making friends — Kevin is a bit of a loner, an 'oddball'. How do you think he became friends with Buzz and Jenny? In a group of six to ten, improvise Kevin's first day at Secondary school when he meets Buzz and Jenny.

f   Different backgrounds — Buzz and Jenny come from very different families to Kevin's. In small groups discuss the type of families these might be, how many children, what their parents do, kind of street and house they live in etc. In groups of three or four improvise a scene or scenes in which Buzz and Jenny are discussing arrangements for a birthday party and who should come, with their respective families.

g   Other people's parents — Improvise the scene or scenes in which Buzz and Jenny's parents come to collect them from the police station after the rescue from the caves.

h   Classmates — How do you think the children's classmates reacted to their adventure? In small groups improvise a scene around the children's return to school — e.g. Buzz with his mates, Jenny with hers, the first class they go to with Mr Butler.

i   What makes us lie? — We all tell lies at one time or another. Think of recent examples in your own life. In the play Kevin lies a lot. Look at the lies he tells and discuss why he does it. Take one or two of the incidents from the play where he does this and in pairs, with one person speaking Kevin's words and the other person being his 'inside self', show what makes him tell these lies.

THE CAVES

We tend to think of caves as natural phenomena, carved out of
rocks by the action of water and waves. Yorkshire's great
limestone cave systems, such as Ingleborough, Gaping Gill and
Stump Cross Caverns, are probably the best known in Britain.
What few of us realise is that there are many cave systems, not
made by Nature but by people, and not out in the wilds but
under, or close to, our towns and cities; Nottingham, Stockport
and Chislehurst are just three examples.

The Chislehurst and Nottingham caves go back, it is thought,
to at least Roman times. Part of Chislehurst's 22 mile (35 km)
cave system is called the 'Druids', and is believed to have
been used by Druid priests for religious ceremonies and even
human sacrifices. During the Civil War, in the seventeenth
century, Royalists fleeing from the Roundheads regularly used
Chislehurst caves as a hiding place or as a cache for their
treasure. Half way along one passage the Royalists dug a pit and
stuck stakes in it to impale any pursuing Roundheads.

The Stockport tunnels, started in the sixteenth century, were
constructed as conduits to bring water from the Mersey river to
two local corn mills. By the eighteenth century some inhabitants
of Stockport had extended their homes by hewing out two-storey
'apartments' in the soft red sandstone on which they stood.
These were later occupied by the 'Navvies' who came over from
Ireland in the early nineteenth century to work on the waterway
systems.

The Nottingham caves, which stretch for miles under the
ground as far as Sherwood Forest, and the Stockport caves were
both well used by the townspeople. Apart from occasionally
being used to live in, they often provided refuge for religious
fugitives and robbers. It was also common for taverns to hollow
out the rock to make cellars and even brewhouses. The remains
of cockpits and bearpits have been found and Nottingham even
had an underground tannery.

During the Second World War both the Chislehurst and

Stockport caves were used as air raid shelters. The Stockport caverns had bunk bedding for 2,000 a night and the Chislehurst caves could accommodate some 15,000 people — the biggest air raid shelter in Britain! The cave-shelters became small villages with catering, sanitary and social facilities laid on. Chislehurst even had shops, churches, a hospital, cinema, dance hall and gymnasium. The rules of the shelter were enforced by 'Cave Captains' and included one that 'Children should be in their pitches (beds) by 9pm and stay there'!

Nowadays these caves are either blocked up or entry is carefully controlled through guided tours because they have become very dangerous. This hasn't stopped some children, like Kevin and his friends, breaking into the caves and risking their lives. Whatever you do — don't try it!

Map of the Stockport Tunnels

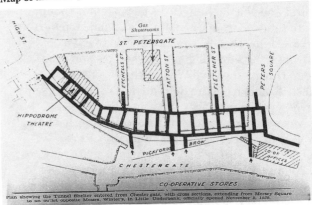

Plan showing the Tunnel Shelter entered from Chester gate, with cross sections, extending from Mersey Square to an outlet opposite Messrs. Winter's, in Little Underbank, officially opened November 2, 1939.

Stockport Caves, which were hewn in sandstone

52

Map of the Chislehurst Caves

Chislehurst Caves – the Haunted Pool

Chislehurst Caves – the 'Druids'

53

The Ropewalk Caves in Nottingham, which had an ornamental entrance (right) and even a stained glass window (above)

THINGS TO DO

These exercises can either be done as a class or in a small group, though some could be done individually.

1 On pages 52–53 you will see two old maps of the Chislehurst and Stockport caves. These are just the sort of maps that Kevin would have been looking at in the library. If there are caves in your area, the best place to find such maps would be the Local History library. You can see on the Stockport map where the tunnels lie under the roads, and where the entrances are. (It doesn't show you all the old features, like the bearpit and 'apartments', which is a great pity.)

- Make a map of your area or town and imagine that there are tunnels and caves underneath. Show where they are.
- Think about the history of your caves. Who built them? What for? Who used them?
- Work out the topography of your caves. Where are the entrances — into people's houses? your garden? the churchyard? the pub cellar? Are any of them secret? How high are the passages? Can you stand up in them? Do you have to crawl at times? Do any of the caves have special features?
- Do any of your caves have interesting names, like Chislehurst's 'Haunted Pool'? If so why? What happened there?

2   Imagine that in one of your caves you find scratched on the wall:

MWG   God   have mercy on my soul   15 October

Who do you think wrote it?

● Write an account of the incident leading up to the inscription being made — you could imagine that you are either MWG or someone who found the inscription.
● In a small group dramatise the story of MWG.

3   Imagine that your caves were used as air raid shelters during the Second World War. (The newspaper articles and photographs on pages 58–59 will show you what it might have been like.) Using as large an area as possible, mark out the caves and tunnels. As a class or group you are going to be ordinary people from your home town who have sought refuge in the caves from the bombings. Divide yourselves into families, neighbours and strangers. Then in character improvise the history of your shelter.
Here are some suggestions:

a   The organisation of the shelter.

b   Two families who hate each other find themselves in neighbouring sets of bunks. What happens?

c   A rather well-off woman finds that one of her rings is missing. In the next bunk is a family whose father is in jail.

d   A birthday celebration.

e   Part of the roof collapses, injuring one person and also blocking off the entrance.

f   A foreign artist comes down into the caves to sketch the life down there. Some of the people think he is a German spy. (This happened to the Polish artist, Felix Topoloski, at Chislehurst.)

4   Your caves have been used by people as a refuge at other times: during the Roman period, when Romans persecuted Christians; when Protestants persecuted Roman Catholics and *vice versa*; during the Civil War; by criminals hiding from the law; by smugglers; by children in Victorian times fleeing harsh employers. The possibilities are endless.

- Dramatise some of these other parts of your cave's history. They may provide names for parts of the system.

5 Most caves have inspired legends or ghost stories. Chislehurst has the ghosts of a Roman Centurian, a hunchback, and an old crone amongst others.

- What ghosts does your cave have? Compile a class book of 'Ghostly Cave Stories'.

6 Page 59 shows two real-life stories of children who found themselves trapped in Stockport's caves. They, like Kevin, Buzz and Jenny, found it a pretty terrifying ordeal. So did Tom and Becky in Mark Twain's book *Tom Sawyer*.

This shortly brought them to a bewitching spring, whose basin was encrusted with a frostwork of glittering crystals; it was in the midst of a cavern whose walls were supported by many fantastic pillars which had been formed by the joining of great stalactites and stalagmites together, the result of the ceaseless water-drip of centuries. Under the roof vast knots of bats had packed themselves together, thousands in a bunch; the lights disturbed the creatures, and they came flocking down by hundreds, squeaking and darting furiously at the candles. Tom knew their ways, and the danger of this sort of conduct. He seized Becky's hand and hurried her into the first corridor that offered; and none too soon, for a bat struck Becky's light out with its wing while she was passing out of the cavern. The bats chased the children a good distance; but the fugitives plunged into every new passage that offered, and at last got rid of the perilous things. . . . Now for the first time the deep stillness of the place laid a clammy hand upon the spirits of the children. Becky said:

'Why, I didn't notice, but it seems ever so long since I heard any of the others.'
'Come to think, Becky, we are away down below them, and I don't know how far away north, or south, or east, or whichever it is. We couldn't hear them here.'
They stared through a corridor, and traversed it in silence a long way, glancing at each new opening, to see if there was anything familiar about the look of it; but they were all strange. Every time Tom made an examination, Becky would watch his face for an encouraging sign, and he would say cheerily:
'Oh, it's all right. This ain't the one, but we'll come to it right away.' But he felt less and less hopeful with each failure, and presently began to turn off into diverging avenues at sheer random, in the desperate hope of finding the one that was wanted. He still said it was 'All right,' but there was such a leaden dread at his heart, that the words had lost their ring, and sounded as if he had said, 'All is lost!' Becky clung to his side in an anguish of fear, and tried hard to keep back the tears, but they would come. At last she said:
'Oh, Tom, never mind the bats; let's go back that way! We seem to get worse and worse off all the time.'
Tom stopped.
'Listen!' said he.
Profound silence; silence so deep that even their breathings were conspicuous in the hush. Tom shouted. The call went echoing down the empty aisles and died out in the distance in a faint sound that resembled a ripple of mocking laughter.

Becky is unable to go on, so Tom sets out for help leaving Becky in the caves. Initially, Tom hadn't thought of leaving a trail to mark the way they had come. Now he searches his pockets and finds a kite string which he ties to a rock, and so he is able to find his way back to Becky when he returns with the rescue party.

- If you had found yourself in similar circumstances, what would you have had in your pockets to help you? If you'd had a compass, would it have worked underground? What would you have done?
- Imagine that you and two friends have decided to explore your local caves. Write an account of your adventures.

7 You might like to create your own play around your cave system.

- Imagine that, like Tom and Becky, a group of children have gone into the caves and gradually realise that they are lost. They are very frightened and argue about what they should do. They huddle together and finally fall asleep . . . Then, a faint sound is heard from a distant part of the cave — what is it?
- You might choose to dramatise the history of your caves through different periods — starting with the Druids and a human sacrifice! In this case the sound coming from the caves could be the ritual chanting of the procession as it nears the sacrificial altar. Who is the victim? Will they escape?
- You might choose to concentrate on one era, like the Second World War and dramatise some of the events suggested in exercise **3**. The sound in this case that the children hear as the past comes alive might be a harmonica or old gramophone playing 'The White Cliffs of Dover', or a distant air-raid siren and bombing.

The best way to approach this would be to break down into small groups and work on the separate incidents, then come together as a class and rehearse the whole, perhaps linking the scenes with appropriate music.

8 The local paper always enjoys a good, dramatic story. Your adventures down the caves are just it!

Take it in turns to play a reporter and interview the others in your group about their ordeal in the caves. Take notes as you do. Then each of you write up your newspaper story.

Ghost train underneath the arches

BUNKS:
Sleeping quarters for more than 2,000

Only a few rust-thin bins, once steaming in discarded tea leaves, remain flaking under make-shift concrete kettle shelves.

Some silent yards down the air raid shelters' sandstone hall sit the ladies' and gents' lavatories, their wooden seats in rotting splinters above parallel sewers in the desperate darkness of this vast network of tunnels.

Chestergate's shelters, which may be opened to the nation after massive restoration as a living museum and tourist attraction, have locked out the post-War world and locked in their memories for more than 40 years.

It is still, shiftless, sandy grotto.

Little exists of life in this incredible network of crude-hewn, arched passageways that were a transitory home to thousands during the Blitz.

Apart from a few honoured visitors, its only guests have been those who entered illegally and inscribed on its water closet walls the thoughts of a permissive society and not one desperate for survival.

Desolate

Surprisingly it is neither cold nor damp. The atmosphere owes more to Blackpool Pleasure Beach's ghost train than a city cellar which it has been since first fully excavated in 1939/40.

Most of its mile-long inter-connecting maze is lined with three-tier bedding of galvanised tubes that slept more than 2,000. Earlier beds, nearest the main entrance, were made of mild steel and are heavily corroded.

These long, bunked galleries are as desolate, compact, strange and still as a London tube in a silent siding.

I had hoped to find the discarded butt of a Craven A. Churchman's or Woodbine to show that the British wartime condition relied on cigarettes as well as fortitude and fraternity.

But most things rot down there. One toilet sign has been eroded into two crusty sections. "Lava" and "tory."

The loos once flushed and were well-lit but privacy was down the drain. Each row sat four, divided by wooden petitions in squat quarters under the curved roof. This really was the bowels of the earth.

Cables and conduits that carried power to the furthest point from Chestergate – 300 yards away at St. Petersgate – still appear in fractured lengths. Most of the ceiling-mounted wooden lamp holders are still in position.

Although the rock was laid down more than 230 million years ago, the caves were very much 20th Century intrusion.

On the other side of the main entrance the chief warden had a makeshift office. The second entrance was a canteen. A little further in there were three bays for first aid and nursing mothers.

The whole of this entrance area, a little eerie though bat, rat and spider-free, has enormous potential for conversion to a "living museum."

Until the plans are drawn up, Stockport's caves will remain a private world, like a sunken vessel.

Drilled to a width of seven feet, the maximum for a self-supporting roof in these conditions, the tunnels were excavated in anticipation of the War and extended three times subsequently.

Most activity, predictably, has taken place near the Chestergate entrance.

One enterprising landlord of a long-demolished pub there, chipped out his own vaults for barrel storage and his stills remain.

ENTRANCE: One of the sealed-up doors

Children trapped on ledge

PLAYTIME DANGER

A HALF-TERM adventure turned into a nightmare for four Stockport boys this week when they were trapped in a cave for two hours as the earth under their feet crumbled away.

On Tuesday evening Michael Stokes, aged 11, Nathaniel Goodier, 14, Nigel Goodier, 12, and Anthony Stokes, 13, from North Reddish, were playing near Norris Towers, Heaton Norris, trying to climb into one of the man-made caves dug into the rocks across the motorway from Debenhams store in the town centre.

Nathaniel, of Chaucer Avenue, Reddish, had managed to reach the cave, but as his friend Michael lowered himself to its entrance the rope he was using snapped and the earth under his feet began to give way. Michael was saved by Nathaniel who grabbed his arm as he fell, stopping him falling 50 feet to the ground below.

Nathaniel's brother Nigel, realising the danger, telephoned his mother asking her to get help.

Shortly afterwards firemen from Whitehill Station arrived at the scene. Using a triple ladder to reach up the cliff face the firemen eventually managed to rescue the boys from the ledge. They were taken to hospital, tired and shaken but were released later that night.

THE four boys return to the scene beneath the cave where they were trapped for two hours.
Pictured (left to right) are Nigel and Nathaniel Goddier, and Michael and Anthony Stokes.

Mrs Goodier told the Messenger: "I'd told the boys to go and play outside. The next thing I knew Nigel rang me saying they were stuck half way up a cliff and for me to get the fire brigade to rescue them."

"We were planning to camp there for the night if we couldn't find a way down," said Nathaniel.

Clive Donohue, Assistant Divisional Officer at Whitehill Fire Station, said: "I thought all those tunnels were bricked up. Some of them stretch back quite a long way. Not only is there a danger that people could get lost in there, they could easily lose their footing and fall. We would not encourage children to play near these areas."

Town seals up tunnels after girls' terror ordeal

Firemen with sledge-hammers freed three Stockport schoolgirls on Sunday from an afternoon of terror, trapped in the pitch-black labyrinth of sandstone caves and tunnels which run beneath the town.

A passer-by in Brinksway heard their screams from behind a bricked up exit and the fire brigade smashed their way through the wall to bring the children out unhurt.

The girls, Susan Gamble, aged 12, of Freemantle-street, Edgeley, Josephine Hart, aged 13, of Castle-street, Edgeley, and Susan Dean, aged 12, of Burrwood-drive, Adswood, got into the caves through a hole in a disused air raid shelter. They went exploring, equipped with three candles, but the last one burned so low that Josephine dropped it on the floor and they found themselves in total darkness.

For almost two hours, they stumbled around the rubbish-strewn and foul-aired caves, feeling the walls to guide them. Frightened and crying, they at last saw a chink of daylight which was coming through a walled-up exit on Brinksway. It was then that a man heard their cries for help.

Susan Dean's mother, Mrs. Joyce Dean, said that the first she heard of the incident was when reporters from the national newspapers had called at her house. She had given her daughter a good talking to.

Early this week, Council workmen were hard at work, re-sealing all the entrances to the tunnels, which were used as air raid shelters during the Second World War.

Borough Surveyor, Mr. Norman Schofield, said the men knew the urgency of the job and that all the entrances would be blocked up as soon as possible.

59

JAILBIRDS

JAILBIRD'S FAMILY

Life at school is not easy for Kevin. He often finds himself on the wrong side of the 'system', and Mr Butler always makes him suffer for it.

But what does he have to cope with at home? His father is in prison, his mother is exhausted from stress, and Tracey, still only 17, works to keep the family together. Kevin's family mean a lot to him — he wants their life at home to be normal — but the pressures are heavy.

Try to find out more about how these pressures affect Kevin by exploring each family character in turn.

Father

Name	Arthur Pelham
Age	42
Occupation	Builder's labourer
	Driver
	Porter

1978   Convicted for receiving stolen goods.
Served 18 months in Strangeways Prison, Manchester.

1982   Convicted for robbery; three-year sentence in Winson Green Prison, Birmingham — reduced to two for good behaviour.

1987   Convicted for burglary.
At present serving a six-year sentence in Wormwood Scrubs Prison, London.

Mr Pelham was sentenced in 1987 for burglary. Imagine that on the day following the crime, this report appeared in a local newspaper.

THIEVES GRAB £50,000

A BIG reward in return for information is being offered by Anthony Austin, who farms near Hoxton, and his wife Aileen, following a £50,000 raid on their home.

While Mrs Austin was in the front garden, and farm workers were in a rear yard, two men ransacked the house. They said their car had broken down – and escaped with £50,000 worth of jewellery. Much of it had been in the family for several generations.

Mr and Mrs Austin of Millstone Farm, hope the reward will bring information leading to the conviction of the thieves and return of the property.

Using this report as a starting point, fill in the details of Mr Pelham's story.

1 In groups of four — improvise the conversation in which Mr and Mrs Austin give their account of what happened to two police detectives.

2 Same groups of four — the farm workers tell the police what they saw of the incident from the rear of the house (exchange roles so that Mr and Mrs Austin now play the police detectives).

3 Following an anonymous telephone call to the police, Mr Pelham and his accomplice are arrested. They both plead their innocence and claim to have an alibi. The police decide to check the alibi of the two suspects by questioning them separately.

Take this exercise in stages:

a The pair playing Mr Pelham and his accomplice work out their story or alibi. This should be done in real detail (perhaps between drama sessions). Try to anticipate the sort of questions that might be asked about the story.

b The rest of the class divide into two groups of police interrogators and question Mr Pelham and his accomplice

c

separately about their alibi, making notes of key facts.

c   Each suspect moves to the other group of interrogators, who must repeat their questioning of the alibi story. Interrogators — you must now look for points where this version of the story differs from the first. *If you see any, do not give the game away to the suspect.*

d   With both suspects sent 'to the cells', the two groups of interrogators come together to compare notes, and to decide whether the alibi is true or false. If you find no inconsistencies in the two stories, then the two suspects cannot be charged with the crime.

e   Call in the two suspects. State whether they are to be charged or not charged, and give the reasons supporting your decision.

4   While Mr Pelham sits in his cell, backtrack in his memory by acting out the following situations that might have occurred some time before he committed the crime:

● In a pub — Mr Pelham meets his mate who has a plan for a 'job' at the farm of Mr and Mrs Austin. Mr Pelham is reluctant at first, but eventually is persuaded.
● At home — Mr Pelham has kept the plan secret, but his wife recognises that he is planning another job. Late one evening when Kevin and Tracey are in bed, she questions him about it.

5   Groups of three — two journalists have been allowed to speak with Mr Pelham while he is in prison. They are particularly interested in ex-prisoners and why so many of them (approx 75%) return to the courts. They want to learn from Mr Pelham the reasons why he felt compelled to commit the crime for which he has just been convicted.

(Journalists: try to ask questions that will avoid predictable responses. Get beneath the surface of Mr Pelham's character.)

When you have completed your interview, write your article for publication.

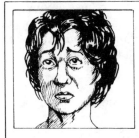

Mother

Name   Gloria Pelham
Age   40
Occupation   Housewife

A prisoner's wife in real life describes how she felt on the day her husband was sent to prison:

> " I came home, collected the children from my neighbour. I didn't feel much like talking; she was very nice . . . I took Sheila to school, and everything seemed quite all right; teachers were quite nice; everybody said, "Hello, how are you?" And I still did not catch on: everybody had read about it in the paper, hadn't they? Everybody knew me at that school; it was like the village school. I come back, and thought, "Oh, everything seems all right." And then my daughter come home from school at the dinner time; she'd ran out of school; and she said, "Mummy, where's my Dad?" And this I really did not know how to answer. "

1   In pairs — act out the scene between two of Mrs Pelham's neighbours. One shows the other a report in the paper of Mr Pelham's trial. They exchange views about why it happened and what the future holds for the Pelham family.

2   A few weeks later, and Mrs Pelham has only social security and child benefit payments amounting to £56 a week to cover all the family expenses. She asks Tracey (who is still at school but has a Saturday job) if she can contribute a few pounds each week. But this would leave Tracey with no money for clothes, shoes, and for going out with friends. Improvise their conversation.

3 Mrs Pelham is falling behind with hire purchase payments on a three-piece suite and a cooker. She goes to see the manager of the company to try to arrange a reduction in payments. She would prefer, if possible, not to reveal that her husband is in prison. In pairs — try this interview.

4 A year later, and Tracey has decided to leave school as soon as possible rather than stay on to take examination courses, even though all her teachers say she has the ability. Kevin has been missing classes regularly and is now implicated in a shop-lifting incident. Mrs Pelham has been asked to come to the school to discuss the progress of her children.

In Groups of four — Mrs Pelham, the headteacher and two other teachers — act out the scene starting with Mrs Pelham's arrival at school.

Tracey

Name   Tracey Pelham
Age   17
Occupation   Shop Assistant

1 Backtrack a year or so — Tracey's careers teacher tries to persuade her to stay on and do A-levels, but Tracey sees a different future for herself. In pairs — improvise their conversation.

2 In threes — two policemen arrive at the door. They are seeking information from Kevin about some shop-lifting in town. Tracey wants to protect Kevin, but at the same time needs to know details of what has happened so she can deal with it, if necessary.

3 Pairs again — in a search of Kevin's room, Tracey finds a box full of cigarettes, trinkets, chocolate bars, etc. Later, when Kevin comes home Tracy confronts him . . .

If Kevin is guilty, should she tell the police, her mother — or keep the secret with him?

PRISON VISITS

We have to start getting ready about two o'clock on the Friday afternoon, and then we have to catch the local bus which takes us to the town. After that we catch another bus to the city on the main-line train route; from there we get the train to London and we usually arrive late in the evening, late for the children that is. Then we catch an underground train and after that a bus, which takes us to where my brother and his wife live on the outskirts of London. Saturday morning we get up, pack our overnight things again, then take the bus and the underground train into Central London. After that it's another bus journey out to the prison.

66 You sit and you have your chat, and usually you stop an hour or more because you've saved up two or three visits so you can have them all at once. Even so the time seems to go very quick, what with all the things you've got to talk about through not having seen each other for so long. You can't think of half of them, at least I never can and nor can he. All the weeks beforehand you're thinking 'I must remember to tell him about this and that and the other'; and then after you've left you remember them all and you think 'Why didn't I remember that to tell him, I'd been thinking of it for weeks and weeks?' But it's too late then, the visit's over and it's not even worth putting in a letter, so that's it. 99

Divide into groups of four — two boys, two girls, in the roles of the Pelham family. A table with two chairs at opposite sides. Prison visiting time. Only one person is allowed with Mr Pelham at a time.

Visiting time is short. Each person will have questions to ask, important things to say, but also things that might be best kept secret. Now act out each one in turn.

- *Mr Pelham and Mrs Pelham.* She is looking much more exhausted on this occasion. Also, she is concerned that they will have to make fewer visits in future as money is short.
- *Mr Pelham and Tracey.* How much should Tracey reveal about her mum — and Kevin?
- *Mr Pelham and Kevin.* Somehow Mr Pelham has learned about Kevin getting into trouble with the police over the stolen property. Should he mention it, try to help him?

JUVENILE COURT

1 At the end of the play the police have not decided what to do about Kevin.

Let's say that he has been prosecuted, and that at the Juvenile Court he has admitted passing on the stolen goods he found in the caverns. Now divide into groups of three — put yourself in the position of the magistrates in the court. You must decide what sentence to give to Kevin. These are the sentences that could be imposed:

- *Absolute Discharge* — Kevin is found guilty but not punished (indicating that the police should not have charged him).
- *Conditional Discharge* — no punishment as long as he does not break the law within a certain period (usually one year).
- *Fine* — maximum £200. As well as deciding the size of the fine, you must take into account Kevin's ability to pay it.
- *Supervision Order* — Kevin will remain at home, but under the supervision of a social worker (1–3 years).
- *Care Order* — Kevin will be placed in a residential community home run by the local authority.

- *Attendance Centre* — Kevin is ordered to report to a centre every Saturday afternoon for six weeks. Activities include physical training and instructions in practical subjects. There may be a journey of about 30 miles to the centre.

2   There are three basic aims behind these sentences in a Juvenile Court:

- to punish — to make the offender suffer in proportion to the amount of harm caused by the crime.
- to deter — to frighten the offender from committing crimes again, and give a warning to others.
- to reform — to help the offender so that he/she no longer feels the need to commit crime.

Which of these aims do you feel is most appropriate in Kevin's case? When you have made your decision, join with other groups of magistrates and, in turn, state your sentence and explain your reasons.

3   In August 1989, the government Home Secretary, Mr Douglas Hurd, proposed that parents of young offenders should be given the same penalties as their children. The idea is to encourage parents to take greater responsibility for their children's behaviour.

The proposal is aimed at young people aged 10 to 17 who are sentenced to a period at an attendance centre. Parents would accompany their children and take part in the programme of practical activities.

- Divide into groups of five. Discuss what you think about the scheme. What are the practical implications? Would it have the desired effect?
- Write a letter to Mr Hurd expressing your responses to the proposal.

It may help first to write down all the arguments for and against.

- Alternatively, write a letter to the journalist Lynda Lee-Potter of the *Daily Mail*. She makes her opinions about the scheme quite clear in the article on page 68. Do you agree with them? Whether you agree or disagree, your letter should include arguments to support your point of view.

Lynda Lee-Potter

The guilty parents who are ruining Britain . . .

DOUGLAS Hurd has decided that parents of delinquent children should be forced to share the sentences of their wayward children.

Magistrates will be given the power to order mothers and fathers of juvenile offenders to go along with their miscreant offspring to sessions at corrective centres – and it's the wisest move the Home Secretary has ever made.

He is finally, and none too soon, putting the blame for vicious children where it fairly and squarely belongs, which is on the parents.

A child doesn't go to school until he's five and by this time he's unconsciously learnt some powerful lessons. Whether they're for good or evil, for compassion or cruelty, is dependent on the influence and example of the family.

Because what an absurd alibi it is to say we live in violent times and children reflect society. If we'd followed this philosophy in the past we'd still be living in caves and roasting an ox over an open fire with men dragging their wives through forests by the hair.

The strength of parents is the strength of a country and if we don't like the way society is going then it's individuals working passionately in their own small units who will change it.

It's up to us to take responsibility for the way our children turn out because the power of the family can combat the world.

Respect

A teenager brought up to respect his grandmother won't mug an old lady, a daughter who sees books and possessions in her own sitting room handled with love and care isn't going to deface a desk.

Politeness and civility in the home is at the root of everything. A son who daily and relentlessly hears his father talk to his mother as though she's less than human is going to have little respect for women, let alone property.

The fundamental truth behind any society that works is that men and women should combine to build homes in which they bring up children for whom they are totally answerable.

It's parents who must love, cherish and rear families with values which will strengthen and help them grow into good and wise and contributing adults.

68

SETTING A BAD EXAMPLE

❝ He says he's changed and he's different, that this time when he comes out everything is going to be OK, he'll settle down and get a job and start working properly, and look after me and the children.

Perhaps I'm a bit doubtful because, to be honest with you, that's what he's said every time before. Each one was definitely the last. He does mean it, there's no doubt about that: but I've always felt he meant it each time before. When he's in prison he's the most reformed man that there is in the whole place; he's been a bloody fool, he's let me down, what must the kids think of him and all that. And each time before, it's lasted a few months after he's come out: then he's off again, down the pub drinking, mixing with all his old mates, starting a job and finishing it the next week, and then ending up back in trouble again.

A few months later

Kevin's father is out of prison and working as a labourer in a warehouse. He has promised to reform and make up for the trouble he has caused his family. Kevin's mother is visibly more cheerful. At weekends Kevin and his dad go fishing or to a football match, and a new relationship develops between them.

Then after a few weeks some of Mr Pelham's mates begin to visit the house. Kevin suspects a new job is being planned. One night his father asks him if he would do him a little favour — a small job taking a couple of minutes at the most. All he would need to do is run along a flat roof, slip through a narrow sky-light (which would be left open), and unlock a side-door from the inside.

● How might Kevin react to his father's suggestion? What should he do now? Consider his options. Make a list of all the things that Kevin could do. Then, try acting out each option in turn with the whole group observing. Discuss each scene — not for its performance qualities — but with the aim of finding the best course of action for Kevin.

CRIMINAL STATISTICS

Statistics show that the majority of adults in prison today were previously juvenile offenders.

> **66** What made me a criminal? . . . Seeing my father, a straight man getting only poverty all through his life for being straight, . . . living in an environment where nearly everyone I knew was dishonest, where stealing was a necessity at times, an adventure at others, but was always acceptable whatever the reason . . . wanting to impress other kids, getting a reputation for being a tearaway . . . seeing the living dreariness of the lives of other people who were 'straight' . . . not being able to face the idea of working for a living because I hated the idea of work . . **99**

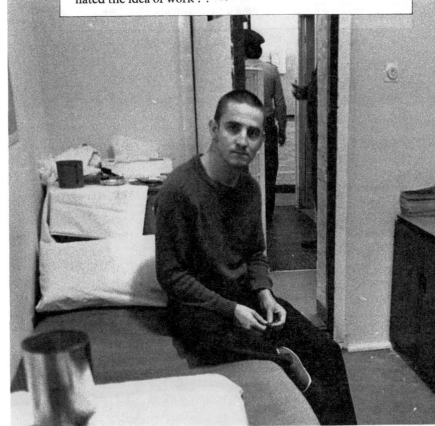

1 This chart shows the number of persons out of every thousand in each age group who were convicted of crime in 1987.

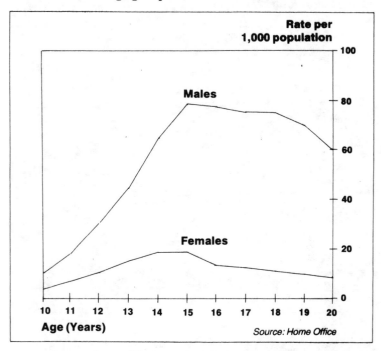

The true figures are in fact much higher as many who commit crimes are never caught and convicted.

Nearly a third of *all* crime is committed by children under the age of 17. In 1987, 6,000 crimes were committed by children under 10.

- The peak age for offending is 15. Can you suggest reasons that would explain this?
- Why do you think many more boys than girls commit crimes?

2 Over the last 15 years there has been a big increase in the crimes of theft:

	1971	1987
Robbery	7,500	32,600
Burglary	451,500	900,100
Theft & handling stolen goods	1,003,700	2,052,000

71

- Part of this increase can be explained by the fact that in recent years a greater percentage of crime committed has been reported to the police. But despite this, crimes of theft are more common now than they were 15 years ago. Why do you think this is so?
- In groups of five — try to identify the reasons why people commit crimes. Make a list of your reasons. Compare them with other groups. Which are the most common causes?

LIVING IN CUCKOO LAND

Kevin makes things up to get himself out of tricky situations. Sometimes it's easier for him to tell a story than admit the painful truth. The trouble is, though, that he has begun to believe some of his own stories, and especially the one of his father as a modern day Robin Hood stealing from the rich to feed the poor.

But his dreaming about the caverns makes more sense. Underground tunnels have existed for centuries and the idea that ancient objects or treasure may be found there is not so far-fetched. This possibility feeds Kevin's imagination so that he gets carried away with his day-dreaming.

All of us, not just Kevin, like to escape now and then from the frustrations of day-to-day living and enter the freer world of the imagination. Certainly, making up stories can be fun.

1 Try these exercises which are all based around the theme of *exaggeration*.

a Divide into groups of 10. Sit in a circle on the floor. Four members of the group, e.g. 3, 5, 7, 10 now take up positions in the middle of the circle facing four other people in the circle.

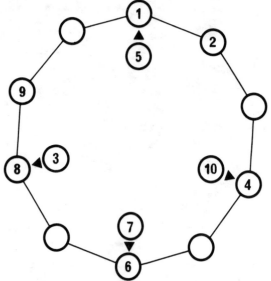

3, 5, 7, 10 begin to tell a story to their partner. The story, 'My Boring Day', starts with the first event of the day — getting out of bed.

After 15 seconds your teacher calls 'All change' and four story-tellers take the places of their partners (1, 4, 6, 8). The partners now find four other people in the circle, sit facing them and:

● tell the story from the beginning and then add a section. In this new section of the story, exaggeration can begin to creep in. Perhaps something a little out of the ordinary happens at breakfast . . .
● after 30 seconds — all change. Again the story is told from the beginning, the new section becoming more and more fantastic.

- after 45 seconds — all change
- after 60 seconds, and so on.

b Groups of four. A & B have just returned from holiday together and talk about their once-in-a-lifetime experience to their two friends (C & D). A & B's story starts in a very matter-of-fact sort of way, but gradually becomes more and more incredible.

A & B — don't prepare the story. Accept and build on each other's ideas during the telling.

C & D — ask questions to draw out detail (you should be suitably amazed and spell-bound).

Everyone must keep a straight face throughout.

c In pairs. Act out an adventure story for two — *as you tell it.*
A starts off:

'The two explorers felt their way nervously along the edge of the ravine . . .'

A & B act it out together.

Now B adds a phrase and the action continues. Try to make the story-telling and the action flow together. If you get stuck for an idea, keep the previous action going till a new idea occurs to you.

2 Have you ever made up a story or altered the truth to get yourself out of a tricky situation? If you have — think back to what happened, and why. What were the consequences?

In groups of three or four — each person describes their situation, the others asking questions.

Take one of the situations and act it out.

Now try to work out alternative courses of action in the chosen situation. What do you think the consequences of each may have been? It may help to act out these situations too.

3 How do we like to think of ourselves? How do we want to be seen by others?

The way we actually are and the way we would like to be seen by others are often very different.

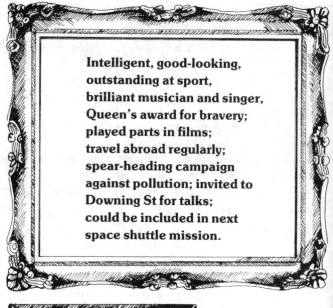

**Intelligent, good-looking,
outstanding at sport,
brilliant musician and singer,
Queen's award for bravery;
played parts in films;
travel abroad regularly;
spear-heading campaign
against pollution; invited to
Downing St for talks;
could be included in next
space shuttle mission.**

Real self

**average at school,
spotty,
enjoy sport – on
the telly.**

Imagine that your *ideal* self has a photo-album of snapshots
recording key events in your life. In groups of six, create a series
of still tableaux each representing one of these photographs.
Compose each picture carefully, paying attention to detail in
both character and situation.

Make up a caption to each 'photograph'.

Pair groups and present pictures.

Throughout the exercise leave one member of the group free
to help compose the picture and to answer questions from the
observing group about each picture as it is presented.

4 *Day-dreaming*

In our imaginations we can 'improve' our experiences and invent
ideal futures for ourselves. This is a useful skill. We need to be
able to think ahead and see how life could be for us. It helps us to
work out what we want to achieve and to know which skills and
abilities we need to develop.

In what sort of situations do you find yourself day-dreaming?

- when bored?
- after a hurtful or embarrassing situation?
- when under pressure?

Write about a particular situation in which you find yourself day-dreaming. Take it in two stages:

- the situation as it really is,
- the dream world or fantasy.

You may find that one gets mixed up with the other — characters from the fantasy entering the real situation, or voices from the real world speaking in the dream.

5 Comics provide ready-made dream worlds. Look through a selection of comics. How do they make their fantasy worlds exciting? Look at the way the sequence of pictures tells a story. What about the style of language used? How are words combined with the pictures?

Sketch a short sequence from a dream-world fantasy using words and pictures as in a comic. Try to create a strong visual impact of danger, mystery, etc.

If you feel your drawing skills are not up to the task, create the sequence through physical tableaux (as in exercise **3**).

6 If you pool your ideas created in the past two exercises you may have enough material for a short play. The drama could be based on a character who finds daily life tough going and who constantly slips into fantasy situations as a way of coping.

Begin by sharing your ideas about awkward real-life situations, and the sort of dream-worlds that may arise out of them. You may find that a basic story line emerges. Put the scenes in a sequence which will create dramatic impact. Now develop your ideas further in action.

Remember — you can mix the real and the fantasy worlds in the same scene, e.g. in a classroom, the central character steps out of his place and speaks to the teacher as *an alien from another planet*. We see the dream in action, but the class (and the teacher perhaps) proceed as if nothing is happening.

7 Alternatively, you could create a play which develops from Kevin's dreaming about the caverns.

Suppose Kevin dreams that during one of his visits to the caverns, he accidentally dislodges some rocks and discovers an opening he has not seen before. It reveals a new passage, not recorded on any of the maps. Inside, the passage is narrow and low, the walls are lined with special stones, each with a pattern or symbol carved on it. With his torch, Kevin picks his way to the end of the passage and into a small chamber — and there, in the centre, is a pile of objects, thick with dust. Kevin has found an ancient hoard of Saxon treasure.

How might the story develop from this point?

Here are some suggestions for scenes to come:

- Kevin takes Tracey down to the chamber, she at first protesting that this is just another of his wild ideas.
- The Press get hold of the story, and Kevin, destined to be rich and famous, is interviewed by a reporter.
- A university archaeologist assesses the importance of the discovery.
- Kevin — now a national celebrity — is the subject of a TV documentary which includes interviews with:
  — his school friends, and,
  — Mr Butler (so proud to have inspired Kevin with such a deep love of history).
- Now able to pay for the services of a good lawyer, Kevin secures his father's release from prison. The Arthur Pelham — 'I STOLE FOR THE POOR' — story can now be told.

- Kevin's mum, fully recovered, shows friends around the new home Kevin has just bought for her.

To build your play you could integrate these fantasy scenes with key extracts from *The Thief*. A good device (though a little unusual) is to decide on your *last* scene first, and then to think *backwards*.

Let's say the final scene is the part of scene 15 where Tracey forces Kevin to face reality:

Tracey — "Believe me, our Dad . . . our Dad's a stupid thief."

At the same time the parallel story of Kevin's fantasy could reach its climax — for example, the reunited Pelham family pose for a photograph in their new home on the day of Tracey's A-level results.

Try interweaving these two dramatic moments.

Now work backwards. Pick out incidents from the play to place along the fantasy scenes. Then arrange them in a sequence so as to heighten the tension between Kevin's real world and his fantasy existence.

Changes from reality to fantasy may need special emphasis. A simple but effective way is to use music — live or recorded — as the play moves into the dream scenes. You may find it works to sustain a low background sound throughout all the dream scenes. Above all, avoid making it seem like a 'technical effect'.

8   Write about a time when you found the truth particularly hard to face. What were your thoughts and reactions?

This may be a very personal piece of writing, so write it as though nobody else is going to read it. Once you have decided what to write about, try to write without stopping, allowing your thoughts and feelings to appear on the page as you remember them.

Having written the piece, you may wish to do a second draft, perhaps in story form with a different setting and somebody other than yourself as the central character. Feel free to change details of characters and events when shaping your story. You may want to show this second draft to your teacher, a friend or 'writing partner', but don't feel obliged to do so — you may prefer to keep it to yourself.

JUMPING TO CONCLUSIONS

Kevin suffers a lot from people jumping to conclusions about him.

Mr Butler
... FILCHING FROM WALLETS, WAS HE? THAT'S ABOUT HIS MARK.

Mrs Pelham
YOU'RE SO MUCH LIKE YOUR FATHER, KEVIN. STOP LYING.

Tracey
YOU'LL END UP IN SOME ROTTEN JAIL.

Buzz
... IT RUNS IN THE FAMILY.

Why do they want to make up their minds so quickly about Kevin? Even his own mother and sister assume the worst. Jenny and Miss Smith are more sympathetic. Rather than label Kevin a liar and a thief, they seek other reasons to explain his behaviour.

1 We sometimes like to express an attitude about a person or thing without really thinking what we mean by it, or whether it is true.

...ERTON ARE ...BBISH.

HE'S A REAL SNOB.

GREASY FOREIGNER.

...IRLS JUST HAVEN'T ...OT THE STAMINA.

Let's look at your own attitudes.

In groups of five — make a list of your likes and dislikes:
- pop stars
- clothes
- foreign food
- schools
- old people
- etc.

Then write down the words and phrases you often use to express your attitudes. Think about *why* you have these attitudes and list reasons for your likes and dislikes.

2 Buzz likes to quote his mum. What sort of attitudes do *your* parents like to express?

HE COURTS TROUBLE
MY MUM SAYS.
HE GOES LOOKING
FOR IT.

Make a list:

- children
- neighbours
- politicians
- the Queen
- animals
- etc.

Make a class survey of the most common parental attitudes. Do some attitudes occur more frequently than others?

3 When we meet a person for the first time we are inclined to make very quick judgements about him/her.
   Look carefully at each of the photographs:

What do the eyes, skin colour, hair style, dress, etc. tell you about the person? Supposing that one of these people is to be your teacher next term, which do you think you might prefer? Write down your reasons why.

Compare your reactions first with a partner and then the whole class.

Many of the dislikes and preferences that people express are unreasonable. There is no real evidence to support them.

Another word for these unreasonable attitudes is *prejudice*.

Our prejudices can make us feel more confident, by letting us know where we stand. Most of us need the approval of others. By sharing popular attitudes we also share the approval of other people.

In this way our prejudices can make clear who is with us, and who is against us.

Prejudice needs constant strengthening. One way of doing this is to seek a scapegoat — someone to blame when anything goes wrong — or just someone to pick on.

83

Scapegoating can occur in families, among friends, between nations — and in school. Observe how people behave in your school playground. What sort of scapegoating goes on there?

Some scapegoating amounts to no more than mild teasing. But it can become aggressive and cruel, especially when people feel threatened in some way. Taken to an extreme it becomes dangerous.

4 The following sequence of statements illustrates the stages by which fear and prejudice can turn into physical aggression.

The scene is a crowded city park on a sunny afternoon.

a 'Look at that green-haired man hitting that child.'
b 'That green-haired man is vicious.'
c 'ALL green-haired men are vicious.'
d 'Look — there's another green-haired man. Hit him before he hits you.' (This green-haired man, who has done nothing to provoke aggression, hits back in order to defend himself.)
e 'There you are, that proves it. Green-haired men *are* vicious.'
f 'Green-haired men will attack anyone.'
g HIT ALL GREEN-HAIRED MEN.

● Divide into groups of seven. Create a series of short 'film-clip' scenes — one for each statement — and each lasting no longer than one minute. The exercise will work best in a large space where you can experiment with a variety of groupings. You may repeat words and phrases, but do not add extra dialogue. The tension of the piece will depend on the contrast between the first scene depicting a peaceful atmosphere in the park, and the final menacing image of people united in physical aggression. Between these two points the shifts in attitude should be made as clear as possible.

5 *Prejudice in the press*

This report, as well as giving some facts of the case, strongly expresses attitudes of the writer.

a Pick out the words and phrases which reveal the writer's attitudes. What sort of attitude in the reader does the report intend to play on?

b Re-write the report from a different point of view. Without altering the essential facts, write the story with the aim of evoking sympathy for David Feeney's parents.

Pet ban for yob in kitten horror

A TEENAGER got a five-year pet ban yesterday for his part in a sick attack on a kitten.

Huddersfield magistrates heard how David Feeney, 17, punched a neighbour's 12-week-old kitten.

The tiny animal was then drop-kicked over a wall into a field.

It suffered several broken ribs and died from internal bleeding, said Steven Pollitt, prosecuting for the RSPCA.

Feeney, of Sullivan Close, Crosland Moor, pleaded guilty to cruelly ill-treating the kitten.

Snubbed

He was also given 100 hours community service.

But magistrates accepted that it was a 15-year-old boy who had drop-kicked the cat.

Feeney had taken all the blame and had been snubbed by workmates, said his solicitor Neil Crone.

He had also received hate mail, including several letters threatening to kill him.

His home had been attacked with mud and stones and his parents had been verbally abused in the streets.

6 *Prejudice in school*

The evidence of researchers working in schools shows that the progress of pupils is affected by their teachers' attitudes towards them.

This confidential report on a pupil was written by his class teacher in the term before the pupil transferred from primary to secondary school.

> Peter seems to suffer from strong feelings of inferiority concerning himself and his work. He has no faith in either. Possibly this is due to parental trouble (mother not living at home) and to poor attainment in the basic subjects. He has, I suspect, been moaned at continually through school life, understandably so, because he is so mischievous. With so little to offer academically, he has only one kind of opportunity of getting into the limelight – that of getting into trouble. He does not make lasting friendships and enjoys working alone. He asked to sit on his own, as he said he worked better. He comes to tell his 'secrets' at odd moments, and obviously worships his dad. Quite a pathetic little personality. I suspect he wants the attention of a mother, and resents it because his own has deserted the family. The mature indifference is probably a cover up for a good deal of hurt.
>
> He finds school work difficult, but has tried tremendously hard this term. His English expression is taking form and he is developing a pleasant style of handwriting. His maths is shaky, and he has been working on bases. He joins in oral discussion and he is knowledgeable concerning a wide range of subjects. I like him, but he needs sympathetic but firm handling.
>
> I have been working away at his basic weaknesses – reading and spelling – and have been encouraging him as much as possible. When he realizes that he can do something really well, then I hope his attitude will change.

a Read through the report again, making a list of all the aspects of Peter's work and behaviour it refers to.

b In small groups discuss these questions:

- which aspects of Peter's development does the teacher consider to be most important,
  quite important,
  not important at all?
- What does the report tell you about the teacher's attitudes to Peter?
  Do you think that Peter's teachers at his new school should read this report, or should they make up their own minds about him?

7   This report about a series of burglaries could be used as a starting point for an extended improvisation focusing on attitudes and prejudice in school.

House raided twice in four days

A HOUSE in Maple Road, St Thomas, has been burgled twice in the space of four days.

The first burglary resulted in the theft of jewellery worth £1,000 from a drawer and the second netted a purse and small amount of cash.

The thief got in through an open back door.

At a bungalow in Somerset Avenue, St Thomas, a thief got into the bedroom through an open window while the occupants were in the neighbouring room and made off with property valued at nearly £2,000.

Thieves broke into a house in Rosebarn Lane during the day last Tuesday. They are thought to have got in through the dog flap and they got away with jewellery valued at nearly £1,000.

Last Wendesday night thieves smashed a window at Lanes Cafe in Marsh Barton and stole £20 from the till. They left £200 damage to the window.

First, you will need some extra 'facts'. Imagine that during police investigations a journalist on the same paper had discovered that at least one of the thieves in each of these crimes either is, or used to be, a pupil at Kevin Pelham's school. A few weeks later the paper publishes a new article bearing the heading:

SCHOOL FOR THIEVES

Ryland Comprehensive

The report names the school, and the pupils and ex-pupils convicted of the burglaries. It criticises the poor state of the building and the 'modern' teaching methods that go on within it.

'WHAT IS WRONG WITH EDUCATION? OUR SCHOOLS ARE TEACHING OUR CHILDREN TO BECOME CRIMINALS.'

Following the report many anxious parents ring up the headteacher, some threatening to withdraw their children from school. Letters are sent to the school, and many teachers are bitterly angry about the way the 'School for Thieves' article misrepresents them and the school. Something must be done. This is a matter for the school governors.

The school governors include:

- the headteacher
- teachers on the staff
- parents
- representatives of the Local Education Authority
- representatives of the local community

It is their responsibility to ensure that the school is doing its job properly in all matters to do with teaching, the progress of pupils, and discipline.

The governors at Ryland Comprehensive are very concerned about the damage to the school's reputation caused by this article and they fear that it will have a serious long-term effect:

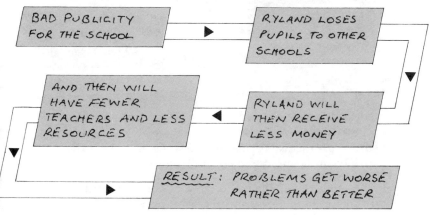

BAD PUBLICITY FOR THE SCHOOL ▶ RYLAND LOSES PUPILS TO OTHER SCHOOLS

AND THEN WILL HAVE FEWER TEACHERS AND LESS RESOURCES ◀ RYLAND WILL THEN RECEIVE LESS MONEY

RESULT: PROBLEMS GET WORSE RATHER THAN BETTER

But attitudes and opinions among the governors about this issue vary greatly.

A special meeting of the governors has been called to decide what should be done.

Before the meeting two of the governors have proposed that the boys involved in the Lane's Cafe theft (see report), who are still in the third year, should be excluded from the school *immediately*.

David Collins   *Age:* 13
Academic record: Good. Likely to choose sciences and languages for GCSE.
Behaviour: Satisfactory. Lively in class. May be easily led.
Father's occupation: Solicitor.
Mother's occupation: Sales Manager.

Lane's cafe theft: Claims he remained outside, but accepted some of the stolen money.

Tony Banks   *Age:* 14
Academic record: Weak, especially in English & maths. Competent in practical subjects. Keen footballer.
Behaviour: Received several warnings. Changed classes in second year to reduce disruption.
Father's occupation: Lorry Driver.
Mother's occupation: Hospital Cleaner.

Lane's cafe theft: First major offence. Admitted breaking window and stealing money.

The meeting must:
- decide whether to exclude David Collins and Tony Banks or to allow them to remain at school.
- draw up practical proposals which will help to improve the behaviour of pupils and prevent delinquency.

Before improvising the meeting, work out the particular attitudes of your characters to these two issues.

Characters

Governors:

Headteacher (Chairperson)

Teachers   Mr Butler
              Miss Smith

Librarian   Miss Waring

Parents

Representatives of the
Local Education Authority

Representatives of the
local community

*People who will be invited
to speak at the meeting:*

Mr Collins

Mrs Collins

Mr Banks

Mrs Banks

Police representative

Social worker

These scenes will help you with the *attitudes* of characters in the
improvisation.

scene 5   — Mr Butler
scenes 7, 12, 20   — Miss Smith
scene 3   — Miss Waring

Work out your character's thoughts on what is best both now and *in the future*:

- for David Collins and Tony Banks,
- for the other pupils in the school,
- for the school's reputation in the community.

Should the school impose stronger punishments? Could links with parents be improved? How might the police be able to help?

Each role could be played by more than one person. In pairs or small groups explore characters' attitudes by:

- asking each other questions.
- acting out situations that might occur before the meeting.
— Miss Smith visits Mr & Mrs Collins to find out more about David's family background
— Mr Banks appeals to his wife to give Tony more attention.

Organisation

- arrange the chairs in a circle.
- your teacher should play the role of headteacher *and* chairperson (normally the chairperson would not be a member of the school staff).
- the Banks and Collins families, police representative, and social worker should sit outside the circle till they are called into the meeting. They will, of course, be able to hear what is said through the 'invisible walls'.
- conduct the meeting formally allowing all characters to express their points of view.

8   Following the meeting. Mr Butler finds an unsigned note on his desk.

> Kevin Pelham was in on
> the Lane's cafe job

It is now two months following the caverns incident and Kevin has kept a clean record at school. But — he *may* have got involved in his father's latest criminal activities. This is for you to decide.

What would Mr Butler do after reading the note? Act out what you think would be his most likely course of action.